AF521950

Bayou Jesus

Bayou Jesus

M. G. Miller

To Everett Johnson —
Best wishes
M. G. Miller

Cavern Publishing Group

ISBN 0-9759896-0-X

Printed in the United States of America.

ACKNOWLEDGEMENTS

With gratitude to the Cavern Press family: my publisher, Tammy Perron, and my editor, Stan Johnson. Thanks also to Cesar Puch for the great layout and design.

Also thanks to Lauren Ball, Roseann Bowlin, Kari Bowling, Velda Brotherton, Cathy Calhoun, Mary Coll, Faye Doege, Denton Gay, Stephen Gooden, Sandie Hamilton, Carl Hitt, Deanna Jones, Brad Keck, Carol Kretzmann, Faris & Linda Miller, Malik & Allena Mitchell, Zola Moon, Tanya Nelson, Northwest Arkansas Writers, Tom & Cindy Parker, Abbie Pfleuger, Dusty Richards, Dr. Michelle Rodgers, the memory of Lois Spoon, Lynn Tankersley and Laura Welch.

Special thanks to Marcus Jeffries, Casey Johnson, Dave Otten and Tim Ratliff, for bringing so much life into mine.

Contents

For Carla

Sunday: 1963

"There it is," she said. "Up ahead."

Until now, Miss Zassy hadn't spoken since I picked her up that warm morning, her gaze on the road as it fell away beneath the tires of my new black Impala.

"Where?" I asked.

"On the left." She motioned toward a thin copse of pines pushed against several open acres. An upward slope gave way to a scrubby lawn, overgrown with neglect, toward a massive oak weeping with the weight of Spanish moss.

I pulled onto the shoulder, shut off the engine, and climbed out, then glanced back at Miss Zassy. Elegant in a pleated navy skirt, she clutched a small brown package in her lap and stared ahead through the windshield. A white cotton blouse, snowy against her arms and neck, clung to skin rich as chicory coffee. Short salt and pepper curls corkscrewed her head, faint lines creased the corners of her eyes, her mouth.

I turned away and followed the low angle of the lawn with my gaze–past the giant oak, the clumps of weeds–to the house. The faded red brick climbed two stories toward bleached olive shutters, cracked and peeling, closed against the light. An earthen-brick verandah stretched the façade, braced by four bone-white and brain-gray columns, exposed for years against the hot Louisiana sun and rain. Bellwether. The place appeared deserted, and that the elements had little regard for its name.

A moment later, I settled beside Miss Zassy again and shut the Impala's door.

"Did ya see anybody?" she asked.

"No," I replied.

"He's still there," she said. "Probably still thinkin about what he done. And I hope he is. I hope he's still reminded every day about the kids." She paused for a moment, then said, "I don't think nobody knows just how young my boy was when it happened."

"How old was he?" I asked.

"Not yet twenty." She drew breath and tapped her fingernails along the plain brown edges of the package. "But I still pray for him every day. I still pray for that man up there in the house, too, all by himself now. I pray that maybe someday God'll find him . . . and wash the blood off his hands."

I reached for the recorder on the vinyl between us.

"Suppose you wanna know everything, don't ya?" she asked.

"If you want to tell me," I replied.

Miss Zassy took another deep breath. "Well," she said, "it's a long way to Breaux Bridge, now ain't it?"

Part One

Father

I

Louisiana: 1917

Zassy was first to spot the traveling man that hot August day. Small for thirteen, her eyes swirled like twin opals set behind sleepy lids, tight black curls bundled under a faded red bandanna. Oblivious to the dark faces bent to the earth in labor and the quick shadows racing across the soy field from the clouds overhead, she made her way to the dirt road, where the traveling man stood beside a black, four-cylinder Lincoln, complete with rumble seat and steel disk wheels.

He towered over Zassy, a dark man of substantial frame, from his generous shoulders to his long legs. Under a battered brown fedora, the evidence of a pockmarked youth lingered in his desiccated yet handsome face, and his jet eyes looked Zassy up and over.

"Why, you're too pretty to be a field hand," he said. "Oughtta be up at the big house waitin on the Missus, pretty thing like you."

Zassy lowered her head to hide the smile.

"Yes'm. Why, you're a house nigger if they ever was. Why ain't you tendin to the cookin and lookin after the babies, girl?" His eyes flashed and his teeth gleamed.

But Zassy couldn't speak.

"Now, you ain't needin to be so bashful with me," he drawled. "Not with Franklin C. Potter. I ain't no wolf, I'm a real ladies man, and I know a lady when I see one, yes I do. Now what say you go on over there and get me a cool drink, huh?"

So Zassy nodded, and ran to fetch him a cup.

"Who's that?" Jolene asked, leaned against the rusted bed of the water truck, large breasts and thick elbows propped on the side rail, her calico dress damp from perspiration. Jolene outweighed Zassy twice over, her hands vises from toil, the bloodlines of Ibo and Hausa flowing in her veins; her eyes mirrored an anguished history.

"Travelin man," Zassy told her.

"Got you runnin for him already, do he?"

"Huh?"

"Travelin men ain't no good, your mama never tell ya that?"

"*He's* a good man." Zassy raised the ladle and splashed water into a battered tin cup.

Jolene cackled.

"Hush up," Zassy said, "he'll hear ya."

"I don't care if he hears me or not. Travelin man's bound to heard lots in his day. Bound to seen and done lots, too."

"Hush up." Zassy turned away and ran at a trot back to the edge of the field. She lowered her eyes and offered him the cup.

"What you two girls goin on about?" Potter's eyes grew animated, his smile impossibly wider.

"She's just crazy, that's all," Zassy said. "She say you ain't no good."

"No good? Now where she come away sayin that about a Bible salesman?" Potter swallowed the water in one great gulp, then wiped at his lips with the back of a leathery hand.

"She say all travelin men's bad."

"She know? She ever been off the farm?" Potter arched his back and laughter rose from deep within, broke free in a hearty bray. "Look at her. Go on, look." He snatched Zassy's arm, spun her around, and pulled her close against him. "See that? What she know about men-folk? I don't know a man alive would give her a second look, do you?"

Zassy tried not to laugh as Jolene regarded them from a distance.

"Course, if a fella's drunk enough . . . ." He chuckled.

Zassy giggled, even as Jolene made her way over.

"What's goin on here?" Jolene demanded.

"Franklin C. Potter," he said, removing his hat. "Travelin Bible salesman. At your service, ma'am."

"Go on, Mister High and Mighty. Ain't nothin special about the likes of you." Jolene seized Zassy's free arm. "Don't you have nothin to do with that trash, girl. You get back to work. And you." She turned on Potter. "Comin around here sniffin up the girls. You get on down the road. Go on, nigger."

"Yes'm." Potter's smile never faltered. "Sure has been a pleasure." He offered up the cup and Jolene snatched it away. "Guess I better find me some gasoline." He pressed the fedora flat on his head and retreated, never once looking back. Long shadows falling across his path, his imposing figure grew smaller on the horizon with his great stride.

Jolene began to berate Zassy, but Zassy didn't hear; she was too busy gazing after the traveling man, remembering what it felt like when he pulled her close and squeezed her tight with his strong, strong hands.

* * *

The day's work finished, the truck filled with girls and women lurched back to the quarter. Pinewood and tarpaper houses surrounded the clearing where a single, tall mimosa stood, chickens pecking at the dirt, a skeletal dog staring from under a porch. Jolene snatched at Zassy's arm. Zassy tried pull away, but Jolene's clutch held tight while the other girls and women climbed down and moved away.

"I'm only doin it for your own good," Jolene said, her voice low, her gaze softened. "You know that, don't ya? Folks like that travelin man ain't no good cause they's one step away from white trash. Niggers like them is the ones to look out for because they's wantin to be like the white folks. And anybody so desperate as to try and be somethin they ain't won't think twice about puttin down on their own kind. Only reason he's lookin at you is because he thinks he's better than you, that you're a easy one to catch. He'll do his thang and wash ya right off him before he goes on down the road to the next. You just taken in because he's payin ya some mind."

Zassy pursed her lips, lowered her brow. "You afraid of him?"

Jolene's clutch eased. "I ain't afraid."

Zassy drew her arm back and jumped from the truck, sending up a small cloud of dust. "I can't spend my life thinkin about things that won't never be."

Jolene grimaced and pulled herself over the wheel well. She took Zassy's arm again, ground her work-strong fingers into the girl's flesh. "Whatta you mean by that?"

"Owww! Jolene! That hurrrrts!" Zassy twisted in her grip, but the more she resisted, the more Jolene's fingers tightened. "Let me go!"

The familiar workaday noises of weary feet and murmured greetings, the strident energy of the children, dissipated. Everyone stared at the woman and the girl in heated argument under the fragrant mimosa shade.

"You think I can't catch myself a man?" Jolene asked.

"Everybody sees ya," Zassy said. "Everybody sees how miserable you are, dressed up Saturday nights for the dancin. And you don't want nobody else any happier than you."

Sunlight dappled Jolene's eyes, her face fell slack.

"Zassy! Jolene!" Zassy's mother, Annabella Cole, approached. "Jolene! You leave her be!" She swiped away a strand of graying hair and wiped sweat from her sun-weathered brow with an apron tied about an ankle-length skirt. "What's this? You take your hands off my girl."

Blood rushed in welcome relief through Zassy's arm.

"Caught Zassy cattin up a feller, Bell," Jolene said.

Annabella leveled her gaze on Zassy. "It true?" Her voice and body grew rigid with embarrassment.

"I just got him some water, Mama."

"Who?"

"Nigger travelin man, Bell," Jolene said.

Annabella grew silent, contemplative. Her eyes lowered with the collective wisdom of motherhood, a lifetime of strife.

"He was thirsty, Mama. It ain't nothin."

"They was makin fun of me," Jolene said.

Annabella closed her eyes and drew breath. "You ain't just jealous is ya?"

"Whatta you mean?" Jolene drew up her wide shoulders.

"Zassy done right by that man." Annabella opened her eyes. "Just because he cottons more to the white man's world than the colored man's don't make him in league with Satan, don't make him any less a child of God. 'We are all laborers in God's eyes', that's the Corinthians. Now go on home and leave us be. And I don't want you comin around makin trouble no more. Some folks thinks when a man's eye don't turn on a girl, her eyes start turnin on her own kind."

Jolene's lips trembled, her eyes narrowed.

"Go on, Jolene," Annabella said, then took Zassy's arm and pulled her toward the far quarter house, its dark grain having never known the feel of whitewash.

Once inside, Annabella said, "Help me with supper, but be quiet, your sister's sleepin," then handed over a tarnished pot and a limp chicken.

Zassy sat in a hard wooden chair. The feathers soon flew in expert rhythm as her fingers dug for the spiny quills. Annabella moved to the grimy window over the basin and stared into the glen of fir and pine.

"Zassy?"

"Yes, Mama?"

"Come here."

She put down the chicken and stood, but had to make her legs move across the wooden floor.

"I wanna say somethin about what I told Jolene." She turned, her face stern.

"Yes, Mama?"

"There's some folks do, women layin with women. The Bible says it ain't right. It's a sin. You be careful of Jolene. Life's done beat her up and give her a mean spirit, that girl. I want you to steer clear, understand?"

"Yes, Mama." Zassy's anxiety ebbed into relief.

"And somethin else. It was good of you to help that travelin man this afternoon, but you steer clear on that account, too. Jolene might be thinkin about things different, but she's right where he's concerned. Understand?"

Zassy lowered her gaze.

Annabella loosed her daughter's bandanna and stroked her hair. Zassy looked up again. Her mother's features had relaxed, and she seemed to gaze into a part of Zassy's soul where she, herself, lived.

"God has blessed me with a sweet child," Annabella said. "I want you to meet a good man some day, and I want you to marry him and have his children. I want you to marry a man that makes his livin off the land, under the sun. That's an honest man. I ain't never told you a lot of things about men and boys. They's things goes on between a man and a woman other than lovin, and I know you know what I mean about that, but there's more to it, honey. There's the kind of love me and your daddy had before he went to the Lord." She paused. "But there's a certain kind of man all that's important to him is the part of lovin you do with your body. That ain't the kind of man who's gonna marry ya. There's a lot of sweet-talkers in this world, and I don't want you to settle for somethin beneath ya. I want you to steer clear of that travelin man if he comes back around, you hear? Men like that get sweet ideas on children when they're roamin from town to town. You find you a good man who's gonna love ya and take up farmin. A man who's got a stake in the land ain't gonna run far, ya hear?"

"Yes, Mama."

"We got lots more to talk about, honey, and we will, but right now help me get on supper."

"Yes, Mama," she said.

Zassy lay awake late that night, long after eleven-month-old Sister May stopped thrashing beside her in bed, long after all sounds in the quarter became the peaceful thrum of cicadas and crickets. She peered into the dark, felt an unfamiliar sensation race up her thighs, and creep into the secret place between her legs. When she did manage to close her eyes, she saw him, painted behind closed lids, etched in her mind. His fingers caressed her below the swell of her tiny breasts.

Franklin C. Potter, at your service, ma'am.

But next morning, his automobile had vanished.

Zassy tried not to think about him. She bent to pick the hard shells from the green stalks, filled three baskets in less than an hour, and hauled them back to the truck for cracking and shelling. The sun flamed without mercy at her back, fueled the fire within, made her aware of the way her thighs felt against one another, dewed with sweat.

She ate lunch alone in the shade of a giant willow, pushed against the field's northern boundary. Enveloped by the yellow blooms and thick perfume, the breeze stirred cooler here, and helped quench the morning's fire. However, white heat still leapt through her arms and legs. It took a man to make a woman feel like she did, a handsome man like Potter. She didn't want any no account plain nigger boy from the fields. Potter excited her because he *was* a traveling man, and she'd dreamed of being free to travel herself. But Mama always told her to stop dreaming.

You're just like Jolene, Mama. You forgot what it's like to be young.

Zassy closed her eyes and leaned against the willow. Her arms ached from work and emptiness. If Potter were here to fill them, he'd ease the pain. He glistened for her: his teeth, his eyes, his life–a life lived moment to moment, where unfailing hope was the most blissful state of being.

Franklin C. Potter. So many wonderful curling letters and hard, straight lines in his name. Last night, after supper, she'd scribbled it over and over inside the back cover of her primer. But what did the 'C' stand for? She'd turned over so many names: Charlie, Caleb, Clarence. But none of them seemed to fit. Then she decided it must be Christian because he *was* a Bible salesman, and Christian could be long for

Christ. Besides, he certainly had the makings of a savior.

The high call to work floated from the fields and died on her ears.

"Come back," she whispered. "I trust you."

The clamor from church floated through the trees and whispered in the window where Zassy brushed her hair, tried to straighten the tight curls on her head. But it didn't work. She couldn't shake the kinks loose and train them to hang straight. She gazed into the mirror frosted with seasons long past, and eyed her good Sunday dress, a dull brown frock with red gingham piping. Mama had sewn a big red bow on the bodice and Zassy hated it. She looked back to her face and startled to see the eyes staring back. They'd aged and betrayed her. A premonition? The kind Mama Lena had?

Famous for reading the cards, Mama Lena's hair and eyes resembled the color of a white man's flesh, looked right into your very soul with a dried-peach gaze. It just wasn't right. Yet, Zassy had overheard Ruth Blackwell one hot afternoon saying Mama Lena told her about a mysterious man coming into her life, and lo and behold, not two months later, Luther Spees joined up at the farm and took a fancy to Ruth. There wasn't much mysterious about Luther, though. He was slow, but a man nevertheless. The only mystery about Luther was how his mind worked–or didn't work. Sometimes Zassy could look him straight in the eye and she just knew he wasn't really there: that wide, vacant stare, ignorant of the world around him, looking right through her as if she weren't there at all, either. But Ruth loved him, and that's what mattered. Zassy wondered if Mama Lena could tell her about Potter, but then she remembered Ruth had had to take a chicken as payment, and Annabella would know if any turned up missing.

Zassy's eyes grew young again, but while the girl in the mirror looked like her, she reflected white, her hair long and straight. Beautiful. She blinked. The pretty girl disappeared. Ugly Zassy stared back. She tugged the brush across her scalp, hating the coarseness of so much thick black hair, and stroked harder until her eyes watered.

"That's how you look best," she whispered to her reflection. "All blurry." She snapped the red bow from her dress and tossed it on the floor.

"You ready?" Annabella called from the doorway.

"In a minute, Mama."

"Get that look off your face and come on, girl," she scolded. "And what happened to your pretty dress?"

The small white-washed church had no steeple, but a single word appeared over the doorway painted in high black letters: REDEMPTION. Lively chatter from inside seemed to make the very walls vibrate. Warm light spilled from the windows, created patches of gold on the grass outside. Saturday nights and Sunday mornings everyone gathered free of burden, flocked under the Lord's steady gaze and rejoiced in His approving nod.

"Quit draggin your feet, girl, and come on." Annabella wore her best gray dress and carried two fresh berry pies, a well-worn Bible tucked under her arm. Beads of perspiration tinged her forehead and upper lip.

Zassy hesitated, lifted Sister May in her arms, climbed up the steps, and walked into the light.

Gleaming faces filled the hall, all smiles, brows damp, the women with paper fans to cut the air: hot, moist, sliced through with excitement. Wooden benches lined the walls, children dodged between the colorful billows of skirts, around long trouser legs. Food lay heaped on three tables at the far end: red beans and rice, shrimp, fried chicken and pork, rolls of fresh-baked bread, desserts. Nearby, a band had set up: two banjos, scrub-board, a fiddle and a drum. Music was a spirituality in itself; it pulled out one's soul so that it might dance free of the bonds of earth, it brought one closer to God. And this night seemed made for rejoicing.

Annabella placed her pies on a table and took Sister May. Zassy found a group of girls her own age, but she didn't talk. She cast her gaze down to the tops of her scuffed shoes. *Ugly, ugly, ugly.*

Then Brother Jim's voice rang out, high and sharp, but Zassy couldn't see him over the people crushed against the pulpit.

"Brothers and sisters! Brothers and sisters!"

The tide of talk ebbed to a murmur.

"Bless all who enter this house tonight! Jesus Christ loves ya!"

"Amen!" came a mingled chorus.

"Hallelujah!" Luther Spees cried.

"We have much rejoicin to do tonight!"

"Amen!"

"But before we get started, I want everybody to meet a man who comes to us from the road, from the Kingdom of God, spreadin His word."

Curious, Zassy craned her neck to see over the congregation, but all she saw was the top of Brother Jim's head. She gravitated along with the others toward the front, inched past two older girls, and spotted Jolene. Jolene glowered, eyes spiteful under a flat straw hat. Zassy backed away and plunged into the crowd.

"He comes before us tonight a sinner turned to the right hand of God. Travelin has taken him all across this country, and many's the time he's taken a wrong turn, like you and me, away from Jesus, away from His everlastin love. 'Til one night when he'd got so low, he picked up the suitcase full of books he was sellin and started readin. That's when he found out it wasn't just books he was sellin, but the truth. 'Cause them books of his was the Holy Bible." Brother Jim paused, then roared, "God's Word!"

A reverent chorus of 'Amens' filled the room.

"That night, in a motor-hotel room in Kansas City, Missouri, he said he started to feel the love of Jesus come in and hold out His arms."

"Amen!"

"Jesus had come to that motor-hotel and showed him God's love."

"Hallelujah!"

"Welcome Brother Frank Potter!"

"Praise the Lord!" issued from the congregation, so alive with the Spirit.

Zassy didn't trust her ears or eyes. She'd pushed her way to the front and stood in disbelief.

It's him.

She drank him in, from the smart, tailored suit at his broad shoulders, to the lips drawing his dried cheeks into a smile. Her heart beat faster. Too hot. Dizzy and weak.

"Praise the Lord!" Potter raised his hands in a gesture of love and reverence. "Thank you, Brother Jim. Thank you all." He lowered his hands to the podium. "I stand before you today a changed man, barterin for God. I make my livin sellin His Word, the God's honest truth. It's an honest profession, and I know I make a difference in folks' lives every day." His gaze found Zassy's, and he winked.

Potter talked on, but Zassy didn't hear. Her head swam. Each wonderful word he'd uttered seemed to hover on the air, then break into feathery white doves circling everyone's heads. She thought she might faint from the heat in the church and the shortness of breath in her chest.

So she did.

* * *

". . . . Zassy! Wake up! Wake up, honey!"

The voice penetrated the fog, echoing from far away, from the Other Side, the Earthly Side. Zassy willed her soul back to her body and her eyes fluttered. Gasps and sighs of relief came from all around as Annabella's face sharpened into focus, Potter standing tall behind her.

"She's all right!" he cried.

The murmur of the congregation escalated in relief.

"Praise the Lord!" Potter smiled and raised his arms. "This child's been slain in the Holy Ghost!"

"Hallelujah!"

Annabella dabbed at Zassy's face with a cool, wet cloth. Potter offered her his hand. Zassy mustered the strength to reach out and take it. He pulled her to her feet and she swayed against him, dizzy, weak in the knees. Helpless. As warm in his embrace as it must surely feel in Jesus' arms.

He leaned close and whispered in her ear, his breath warming the goose flesh at the back of her neck. "That was just perfect, honey. Now everybody's gonna want a Bible."

When everyone settled into the rhythm of the music and the line to buy Bibles, Annabella insisted Zassy go home and rest.

"No, Mama. I wanna stay."

"No, now go on home."

Zassy stamped her foot.

Annabella pulled her into a corner away from the dancing couples and the beat of the music.

"You straighten up and go on home." Her eyes narrowed. "I'm keepin your sister with me so you can have some peace and quiet. Enjoy it while you can, girl. Probably the last you'll get before you're in the grave."

"Yes, Mama." Zassy sighed. Mama still didn't trust Potter, although he'd more or less caused a miracle. She turned away, saw him surrounded with frantic hands eager to relinquish dollars for Christ, then lost herself in the warm sea of faces. Jolene stood near the entrance, lips drawn into an uneven smirk. But Zassy looked away, walked right past her, then ran home.

The kerosene lamp burned low. Zassy fell onto the mattress, stared into the gloom, listened to the faint strains of music haunting the air under the insistent, hollow grumbling of thunder.

"I hate you, Mama. I really, really hate you." She rose from the mattress and leaned on the windowsill. Heard music. Voices. Laughter, too.

Lightning flashed. Thunder boomed. Zassy startled at its quake.

"Little girl!" a voice called, set apart from the others. Closer. "Little girl!"

Little girl, she seethed, ready to be angry with anyone. Then she recognized it. *It's him.* She pulled herself up, bent low to avoid the window frame, and the next instant her feet hit the ground outside.

"Little girl!"

"Here!" she called.

"Where?"

"Over here!" She jumped, flailed her arms.

"I can't see ya!"

"Here!" Her heart pounded double-time, breath ragged, much as in the grips of that religious fervor earlier. She trembled, peered into the inky black, saw him float toward her like a ghost. Her legs wouldn't move. Her throat closed tight.

"That was some time, huh?" he said, so close now she could touch him.

But Zassy couldn't speak.

"You're the sweet thing got me a drink the other day, ain't ya?"

"Uh-huh," she breathed.

"Was you really touched by the Spirit back there?" he asked.

She didn't reply.

"Well, was ya?"

"Yes," she whispered. But touched by whose spirit, she wasn't quite sure.

"I meant what I said, you know, the other day, about you bein a pretty girl and all." Potter's words flowed like silk. He moved closer. "How old are you, girl?"

"Thirteen." She hated herself for telling the truth.

"Hmm. Thirteen's a good age," he reflected. "Most girls lookin for a man by the time they're your age. Suppose you already got about ten, twenty fellers, ain't ya?"

"No."

"Whatta you mean? You ain't got no boys crawlin after ya? Shit. Boys around here must not know their hind-end from a hole in the ground. I think you're somethin mighty special."

"Me, too," she said. "I-I mean, *you*, too."

He pressed against her, his rough fingers reached up to stroke her chin.

"You mind if I was to kiss ya?" he murmured.

She whispered, but her words faded under the thunder.

"What'd you say, honey?"

Was this love? Flashing like lightning. Driving like thunder. Love, freeing the spirit, yet stretching the body tight as a drum. She thought it was. Zassy pulled him tighter against her, oblivious to the first fat drops of rain, the rough wood at her back. A sudden deluge soaked them through in but a moment.

This is love. A wet, hard river carryin you along to empty into the ocean.

She pulled away as lightning flashed and thunder

crackled, then led him to the porch, where they both laughed, shaking water from their clothes and hair.

"Mama won't come home 'til it stops rainin," she said.

"Amen!" Frank replied. He stepped into the milky yellow glow and stripped the shirt glued to his chest before the screen door banged shut behind him.

How it delighted Zassy to feel the squirm of wet nerve endings strain and punch against her.

See? See how he wants out? See how he can't wait to take hold of things?

Anxious to tell anyone, she knew she didn't dare.

My baby. My secret.

Bundled under extra layers of cotton gingham.

You're a strong one, she told him in the voice only he could hear. *A fighter, that's what you are. Ain't gonna be a man to take the easy way out. Got a name for you, too. A respectable name. Gonna give you your daddy's. You like that, Frankie? You like the name Franklin Christian Potter?*

It kicked.

Zassy bit her lip.

Don't you worry none, Frankie. Your daddy be back before you're born. He'll be bringin everybody their brand new Bibles. You shoulda seen 'em, all lined up to buy the De-lux Edition. Had to take their orders back to Bossier City, though, so he could get all the names wrote in gold on the covers. But he'll be back, he just had lots of orders to fill, what with all the folks he was plannin on meetin up with in Shreveport. Yes, baby, he's comin back, she said in her secret voice. *He promised.*

Most mornings, Zassy just managed to hang her head over the side of the bed and spew vile liquid into the rusty chamber pot. While Sister May cried. And Zassy choked trying to shush her.

As days turned into weeks and time grew into months,

no sign of Franklin C. Potter–traveling Bible salesman extraordinaire, Savior–came to pass. But Brother Jim continued to speak of him as if he weren't merely a servant of God, but a Saint as well:

"And one day, brothers and sisters, he'll be comin back, bringin those blessed Bibles with each and every one of your names inscribed in gold. As gold as the paved streets in heaven, where each man has his own mansion."

Visions of tall white columns sprang into Zassy's mind as she fidgeted on the pew. *Mansions. Frank'll take me to my mansion.* She couldn't suppress the smile.

Not a single day passed when she didn't think about him, about his body pressed hard against hers. Now that she'd had him inside her, there was an empty space only he could fill. Even as the child within her complained, she bent toward row after row of beans, and thought of Frank. Even as her legs and back cried out, she wondered when he'd come to take her away. Even as the child within her begged for food, she ate for Frank, too.

Gonna give him a healthy baby, I am. Gonna give him a strong son to carry on his name. Won't he be so happy when he finds out? Won't everybody be so happy for me, for all of us? Come back, Frank. Make an honest woman out of me before anybody finds out. Give your boy a daddy before folks start usin that ugly name on him.

At night, Zassy found a quiet clearing in the woods and climbed up onto a low mimosa branch. Some nights, she merely absorbed the sounds–the belch of bullfrogs, the hum of insects, the hollow call of cranes–and digested them for her baby: *That was a cricket, Frankie, hear that?*

Some nights, she talked to him about that big white mansion and how wonderful everything would be behind its doors: *You want lots of brothers and sisters, Frankie?*

And some nights, she talked to him serious:

That's what it sounds like when folks is laughin and havin a good time. See the fire? Built up a good one tonight. Probably all sittin around it drunk by now, though. Don't you never do that, Frankie. Don't you never start drinkin.

She just knew he swam around inside her with his ear pressed close against her heart, because that's where all her words came from.

Eight months passed. Still no sign of Potter. And eyes turned on Zassy more than ever. At first she wondered if anyone noticed her quick with child, but then decided she was worrying for nothing. She didn't show that much, especially when she sucked in her stomach. Mama had chided her for getting fat, however, and told her she'd better slow down or she'd get as big as Jolene. Thank God Mama would never have expected It of her.

Soon, Zassy began to believe that all the others who stared at her, the girl so blessed with the Spirit on that night so long ago, were really looking to her for an answer. Had God told her when the traveling man would return with their Bibles?

She prayed every night, but no one answered, and her thoughts turned again on Mama Lena. Could she tell her when Frank would come back?

A night came late in March when Zassy sneaked down to the witchy woman's shanty near the water. She saw a girl she didn't know walk up to the door in the moonlight, saw the door open, and the girl disappear inside. Shadows moved behind closed curtains, the lights dimmed, a soft glow came from within. Quiet for so long, Zassy nodded off. She curled into a ball to protect her baby and let the familiar cadences of eventide lull her into peaceful slumber.

Laughter startled her awake. But the flicker of firelight through the trees told her it was only the men around their fire trying to out-lie each other.

Zassy pulled herself up, brushed the leaves from her skirt, and glanced toward Mama Lena's. Dark. Only the shack's uneven shape outlined against the moonlight.

Glass shattered behind her. More laughter followed. Above the uproar, she unmistakably heard Luther Spees.

"Brother Jim say he's comin back, don't you believe it?"

"I think y'all are a bunch of goddamn idiots," another, unfamiliar voice replied. "That feller outfoxed ya. He ain't comin back."

"How you know?"

"Because there ain't no book printin place in Bossier City. I checked."

It ain't true. It ain't.

Numb, Zassy stared into the mirror in her bedroom. A spring of tears welled behind her eyes, but she refused to let them go, refused to give in, because that meant accepting it. She tried to keep the warm memories alive, tried to remember that blurry wet night and the fire he lit in her soul, but it didn't work.

All the months hiding, pretending, wearing loose dresses. Lying. All the sleepless nights, terrified of being found out. What if Frank didn't come back? What would she do with the baby? What would Mama do? Misery washed over her in a wave, left her sick and scared.

Is this a sign, God? Or is this Your idea of a cruel joke?

The baby kicked.

She pulled the dress tight on either side of her swollen hips and turned sideways to examine her shape in the mirror. The weight of the past months pressed on her shoulders, but there also came a great relief as every muscle, held tight for so long, relaxed. The baby tucked under her ribcage stretched, and she saw convulsions of gratitude.

Soon. Gonna be real soon.

Her gaze wandered over her face, down the length of her swollen body, and up over her shoulder.

Where her mother stood.

Annabella's face hung slack. The black shock in her eyes turned the color of rage.

"Whose is it?" she choked, the energy for her voice burning instead as flames in her eyes.

The air began to spin in a stale whirlwind. "P-Potter," she could only whisper.

Annabella didn't speak for a moment, but finally she said, "I can't forgive this, Zassy. God won't, neither. You're gettin rid of it."

"No, Mama!"

"You're gettin rid of it, understand?" Annabella stepped forward and slapped Zassy's cheek.

The sharp sting, coupled with an utter helplessness, brought immediate tears to Zassy's eyes. "No, Mama," she whispered.

Annabella raised her hand to strike again.

But Zassy ran. Past her mother. Out the door. And into the night. Ran into a formless and empty darkness, where pain gripped her soul, and burst through the numbness of her body to settle in her belly. God's punishment. The very pain with which He'd smitten the first woman. The child within her shook. Zassy bent double and cried out.

The underbrush rustled.

"Lord have mercy," came a familiar voice. "What's goin on?"

"Jolene! Help me!"

"God in–" Alarm rose in her voice. "What's–?

"Mama!" The storm in Zassy's belly intensified. *Are you really comin now, Frankie? Now?*

"What about your mama?" Jolene stepped closer.

"I'm havin a baby!" Zassy wailed.

* * *

The stable crumbled with neglect. Hard times had broken up the acreage, and this plot had become an undisputed territory forgotten in the rush to save the farm from financial ruin. The ground squelched under Jolene's feet as she carried Zassy through the fir and pine toward the darkened structure.

Inside, the loft sagged with time and rot, but a small amount of dry straw was tucked under one of the fallen beams. Someone had slept there recently and reinforced the wood with several rough-hewn timbers and twisted nails. Jolene laid Zassy gently on the straw, but a moment later, the girl cried out.

"Hold on!" Jolene said. "I ain't ready yet!"

But the child was. Zassy screamed, and within moments, he sprang from between her legs with a wet, gaseous sigh.

"It's so dark I can't tell if it's a boy or a girl," Jolene said.

"It's a boy," Zassy whispered.

Jolene wrested the pulpy rope in two, spread her skirts over the straw, and laid the baby on top to tie off the fragile cord. She lifted him to her breast, moved to the stable door, into the moonlight, to regard the legs kicking at the world into which he'd come.

"It's a boy!"

"I know," Zassy whispered.

"Who's it belong to?" Jolene laid the baby at Zassy's side and stroked the thick black hair on his head.

But Zassy was busy counting, feeling for his fingers and toes. *Ten.* She melted into the straw.

"Whose is it, Zassy?"

But the night came down around her with a gentle

black rhythm, and pushed her along a dark, dark stream. "It's God's." She drifted deeper into the tide of unconsciousness. "It's His."

"You're talkin out of your head," Jolene said.

"Mama," Zassy mumbled. "Won't let her . . . give him away. Help me, Jolene. I want my baby."

Jolene rushed home, gathered scant belongings in bundles, a change of dress for Zassy, and blankets for the baby. Daylight brought urgency, and she hurried back through the woods. Fog crept along the ground, nestled at the base of the trees. A brilliant burst of red erupted from an unblinking eye hovering on the horizon. The fog captured its fire, crystallized the light, as well as Jolene's future.

Was this fate? One that didn't include the loneliness of the past twenty-three years? A child would change everything between her and Zassy, bind them. Always looking out for him, for each other. Always together.

"Come with me." She bent to embrace Zassy and pull her to her shuddering legs. "I'll take care of ya."

And they fled the stable before the sun climbed higher, little evidence left in their wake but for the bloodstained straw.

"Where we goin?" Zassy asked.

"I don't know," Jolene said. "The Promised Land, maybe?"

They traveled south, slept on bundles of clothes tied in sheets. Jolene forgot to pack needles and thread, so she tied her hand-me-downs about Zassy's waist with strips torn from a pillowslip.

"Don't you worry none." Jolene drew the dress tight around Zassy's hips. "I'm handy with a needle. Next store I see, I'll buy some. And get lots of thread, too. I'll fix you up, girl. I'll take care of ya."

At night, under a wool blanket tied between two trees for a makeshift tent, Frank lay between Zassy and Jolene for warmth. Jolene cooed and gurgled over him, offered a doughy finger for him to clutch.

"Hush, Frankie," Zassy said. "Mama's here."

"Why you give him that name?" Jolene asked.

"Because it's his daddy's."

"His daddy's no good. He might have fooled everybody else, but he ain't fooled me. Besides, you can't treat people and God the way he does and get away with it. You shouldn't give him the name Potter, neither, like y'all's married or somethin."

"He's gonna have his daddy's name," Zassy insisted. "I always known it. Don't laugh. I always known what his name's gonna be. Just like I always known he's a boy."

Some nights, curled in the crook of Jolene's arm, Zassy dreamt. About an angel. With her mother's face. Come to take her baby away. And some nights, she dreamt about Frank, about being married and living in that big white mansion. However, the picture grew hazier all the time; she couldn't make out the details anymore. And sometimes, she couldn't even remember his face.

For two weeks they wandered deeper into the Delta. The floodplain's soil grew rich, ripe for cotton and sugarcane. Jolene had little money, and it dwindled fast. She bought or stole bread and eggs, needles and thread, a pair of scissors, and spent an entire afternoon altering a gray dress to fit Zassy.

"Stand up. Let me look at ya."

Zassy stood, turned side to side, twirled the skirt in the hazy sunshine. "This is right pretty," she said. "Thank ya."

Jolene lowered her gaze, delighted and embarrassed by all the unfamiliar attention.

"I mean it. If it weren't for you, I don't know what me

and Frankie would do."

"But I wanted to help."

Zassy planted a kiss on Jolene's head. Jolene closed her eyes, her heart caught in her throat. She lived on it for days.

At times, the occasional automobile puttered by the trio. Twice they hitched rides with truckloads of mournful black faces: migrant farmers and their tribes. And during those miles down the road to nowhere, no one talked, they only stared at the child in Zassy's arms.

Frank only cried when he was hungry or needed changing, but that was a great deal of the time.

"I can't do it." Zassy sighed.

"Just you remember," Jolene admonished, "he's your baby and you got a responsibility to take care of him. You make him a fittin mama. You be good to that baby and he'll be good to you." She looked into Frank's eyes. "I feel for him. He's somethin special. He brought us together, ain't he?"

"That was sweet of you to say." Zassy smiled. "I told you he was somethin special." She pulled the hair away from her neck with her free hand, turned away, and gazed out over a broad expanse of clear-cut field. A cold mist collected on the air, and transparent waves undulated over the wounded earth. Zassy lowered her hand, her gaze, her voice. "Hatin myself just about wears me out sometimes."

"Why you say somethin like that?" Jolene asked.

Zassy turned back to face her. "Well I do. Don't you ever hate yourself, like, for bein too fat or somethin?"

Jolene's mouth drew tight.

"I'm sorry," Zassy said. "I never did mean to be hateful, I just don't think about things before I do or say 'em. I know it's better to love somebody than to hate 'em. Hatin other folks just about wears me out sometimes, too."

"Who do you hate?"

"I don't know," Zassy replied. "Everybody. Nobody."

Frank began to cry. Zassy pulled a swollen nipple

from her dress, poked it into his mouth, and looked up. "You forgive me? I didn't mean it."

But Jolene didn't answer. Frank was staring at her. A strange weightlessness, an utter peace, bloomed all around her, and the sensation of her feet leaving the earth was very real. Blood pounded behind her ears. She closed her eyes.

"You all right?" Zassy asked. "I really am sorry."

"What?" Jolene's voice was light as the breeze caressing the rended countryside. She opened her eyes, saw Frank still staring at her.

"You believe me, don't ya?"

"What?"

"You believe I'm sorry, don't ya?"

"Course I do." Jolene stroked a finger across Frank's cool cheeks. But warmth seemed to gather from his extremities, focused into a single beam of energy at his chest. To touch him was the sweetest sensation. Love, acceptance, and a strange salvation radiated from his pure, new heart. Not in all the days of her life had she imagined the touch of another human being inducing such exaltation. Her senses were raw with delight.

"Jolene! I said I was sorry!"

Jolene blinked. Looked up. "I forgive ya," she said. "I remember what it was to be as young as you are. I had an unthinkin tongue, too, but mine was hateful from bein lonesome, you know what I mean? Not havin people to talk to except yourself, and even then hatin yourself so much that the only words ever come out was spiteful?"

Zassy only stared.

"If you want me to, I'll stay on and help ya." Jolene gazed again at Frank. "I wanna be near him. For a long time." She peered back into Zassy's wide eyes, mirrors to her own desperate soul. "I wanna stay with you, too. That all right?"

Zassy smiled. "I want you to stay," she whispered.

* * *

For several days, Zassy and Jolene traveled south along the Calcasieu River. A cold fog rolled off the water every morning to awaken them with a sense of being displaced, lost, of having been devoured by an unknown beast. And each day their journey began with a blind sense of faith. Jolene felt sure Frank would give them a sign and lead them out of the wilderness, sure she'd feel it in her heart when they came upon the Promised Land. However, their stomachs led them to the city where the river grew wide. Lake Charles looked promising simply because it was there.

The plantation house shimmered amidst the pines, the air thick with noonday heat. Four columns braced the earthen brick veranda. Wisteria and bougainvillea climbed along the faded red brick, pink and white buds bursting against green-shuttered windows.

Alert to any movement, the women made their way across a vast expanse of haphazardly manicured lawn. The stillness was unsettling, even in the daylight. Jolene tried the back door. It opened. "Stay here," she said, and disappeared inside.

The sun from the high windows reflected off polished surfaces: marble, copper, brass, iron. A silver door caught Jolene's eye, a large walk-in pantry. She skirted the tile toward food and salvation, opened the latch, and peered inside. Row after row, floor to ceiling, enough food to feed a family for at least a year: tin cans and glass jars of fresh preserves, twenty-pound sacks of flour, a stockpile of sugar rations, row after row of boxed goods. She reached for a jar of peach preserves as movement came from behind. *Zassy?* Jolene turned.

And met with the gleaming tip of a broadsword. She couldn't find the voice to cry out.

"What do you think you're doin, woman?" came a

nasal whine.

Jolene's gaze raced down the blade to the nervous little white woman, hands unsteady from the weapon's heft. Shorter than Zassy, but much wider, pale gray eyes wide in alarm, unruly strands of salt and pepper hair hung past her double chin to rest on the shoulders of a rumpled blue house dress.

"We was– I–"

"Just you get on out of here. Haven't we done enough for you already by settin you free? Now you want to steal from us, too?" The blade wavered.

"We was hungry–we didn't see nobody–we–"

"We? You mean there's more?" Her gray gaze darted about the room.

"It's just me and another girl, ma'am. And a baby. We'll go. You don't need that–"

The little round woman motioned to the door with a heavy sway of the broadsword, eyes calmer with the assurance of the upper hand. Jolene moved quickly past her. But as she reached the door, the woman said, "Did you say there's a baby?" Still high and firm, her voice was decidedly calmer.

"Yes'm." Jolene turned. "Three weeks old. Been on the road since he's born."

"Why?" She lowered the handle of the broadsword to rest against her ample stomach.

"We need work, ma'am. We need jobs and a place to live so we can take care of that baby proper."

"Where's this girl? This baby?"

"Outside, ma'am."

"Bring him over," she replied, her voice tinged with skepticism. "I wanna see him."

"Yes'm." Jolene opened the door and called out.

Zassy appeared from around the corner, but stopped when she spotted the little woman brandishing a sword.

"It's all right," Jolene said. "She just wants to see the

baby."

"No, it's not all right!" The woman stamped a slippered foot. "It's not all right to just come into people's homes and steal from them. You could have just walked right up to the front door and asked. But no. You have to come sneakin in the back way like thieves in the night. Let me see that baby."

Zassy didn't move, one foot frozen on the stoop. Frank began to cry.

"Show her the baby," Jolene urged.

Zassy took a hesitant step up, and into the little woman's distrustful scrutiny.

"Can I put this thing down?" The blade wavered again, a soft eagerness replacing the shrillness in her voice.

"Yes'm," Jolene said.

She lowered the weapon with a grunt, propped it against a wall, and moved toward Zassy, a full head shorter than the girl. Zassy clutched Frank closer to her bosom before offering him up. The woman took him, rocked him against her breast until he quietened, then turned to Zassy.

"Well, come on in. I'm invitin you this time so it's all right. Get somethin for this scrawny little girl to eat, too. You his mama?"

"Yes'm," Zassy murmured, her gaze never leaving the baby.

"If you're gonna take care of this little one, you're gonna have to take care of yourself, too. There's some ham and beans in the ice-box."

"Thank ya, ma'am." Zassy moved into the kitchen and the bright sun streaming from the high windows.

"Where is everybody?" Jolene asked.

"Off to the war or run away." She sighed. "The girl I have cook and clean doesn't come anymore. Her husband came back wounded and she's takin care of him. There's a man from town, Silas, takes care of the grounds, but he's gettin too old for it. I just don't have the heart to let him go. Marie, that's my nephew's wife–Samson's his name, like out of the Bible–she's in town. They were wantin to have a baby before he went overseas."

"He a soldier?"

"Marine. And I'm Teense. Teense Boudreaux." She smiled. "My daddy named me Teense because I was so small when I was a baby. The way Samson says Aunt Teense sounds like 'Ain't Teensy', and I guess I'm really not anymore." Her double chin waggled.

"Ma'am?" Jolene asked.

"What?"

"Who keeps the place clean for ya and does all the cookin now?"

"I do. That's why I haven't touched the place since Rosa run off, that's why Marie's in town, gettin somethin to eat. She doesn't like to cook any more than I do. It's a shame, really. We just tore down the cook-house a few years back and built on to the main house."

"Well, if I was to say so, maybe you're thinkin about somebody to take the girl's place? Somebody to cook and somebody to clean?"

"You want jobs?"

"Yes, ma'am."

"Both of you? I can't hire both of you."

The air grew thick with defeat until Frank gurgled in Teense's arms.

"Of course, it would be nice havin a baby around." She paused, rocking Frank in her short, beefy arms. "Might help cheer up Marie," she contemplated aloud. "She's been awful lonesome since Samson left. I . . . I could only pay the one salary, though."

"Yes, Ma'am!" Jolene piped up before the woman could say more and talk herself out of it.

Teense hesitated. "Well, we could give it a try, I guess. Maybe you could start by cleanin up after yourselves?"

Jolene nodded and smiled.

"There's a crib upstairs, just waitin on a baby. Might as well be this one, I guess. What did you say your name's were again?"

"We didn't." Jolene chuckled. "I'm Jolene Emory and this is Zassy Cole. This here's Frankie."

"I'm not gonna have to use my daddy's broadsword on you again, am I?" the little woman squeaked.

But neither Zassy nor Jolene replied.

Dear Mama,

I'm fine and so is the baby. I named him Franklin Christian Potter. I love you and miss you and hope we can be together again real soon. Don't worry about me. I'm fine. Me and Jolene got a job in a big house in Lake Charles called Bellwether. The Missus is real good to all of us. We got a room at the back. Jolene cooks and I clean. The Missus don't mind us having Frank around as long as we take care of him real good. We do. I'm sorry for everything, Mama, but I can't be sorry for having Frank. He's the prettiest thing. I wish you could see him. He'll be an important man someday. I know. Kiss Sister May for me and tell her I'm all right.

Love, Zassy.

II

Marie hated the automobile. The new sedan would be less conspicuous, but it sat in Jimmy Hazard's shop on Calcasieu Drive. Something about the brakes. But Marie hadn't the head for mechanics. Samson told her she hadn't the head for lots of things. He was halfway around the world, though, probably sitting in a café on the Left Bank waiting for the next strike. His letters said as long as the boys remained ready to move at a moment's notice, life could be very good in the City of Light; any American soldier could drink free on the French.

Marie plowed through the long, thin columns of the newspapers every day, read about advances and retreats, the gruesome tales of boys rotting in foxholes. Only so much a brain could absorb about war before it started to go numb. Only so much a girl could do to find diversion.

Samson's letters cool and detached, political ambitions made him restless, his thoughts far from the war. The youngest Alderman to sit on the Lake Charles City Council, Samson studied law now and again at Baton Rouge when tired of loafing on his inheritance. Politics bored her. Everything bored her. She was rotting just like that old family plantation. Bellwether gleamed on the outside, much the same as one of her insincere smiles, but the plaster crumbled inside and the foundation was sinking.

Were people looking? Did anyone recognize the car? Always one to draw attention to himself, Samson surrounded himself with pretty things: polished chrome and red leather interior, slim-hipped women and influential faces. And Marie was a pretty girl, that's why he married her, he'd said so:

"I need a woman other men will envy, that other women will look up to. Not somebody too pretty, but fresh-scrubbed in a down-home-girl way. You fit the bill."

The persistent suitor, the endless phone calls, the flowers, finally made her relent and marry him. After all, she fit the bill. Besides, she didn't know what she'd do when her mother drowned in the consumption. She was all Marie had left after daddy– Yes. A husband seemed the most practical choice.

Slim-waisted and narrow-hipped, Marie's small breasts were just ample enough to coax into show if she wore the right brassiere. This day, she wore a black cotton blouse and a dark blue pleated skirt. Didn't want to stand out. Blonde hair curled toward angular cheekbones, the blue of her eyes waned. She hadn't slept well the night before, and the lack of it showed. *He's not gonna want me anyway. Not now.* Her fingers tightened on the wheel: rigid in her hands, hard to steer. Like the direction of her life. She was twenty-five years old.

Marie saw the Westlake shanties first: small, hastily built shacks formed with the hands of unskilled labor. Colored men and women sat on their porches, faces slack and worn as their dwellings. Dirty children played amidst the squalor of broken glass, discarded wood and nails, and heaps of twisted metal. Marie looked back to the road. She didn't want to see it. There would be a time for caring later. Right now, she had other things on her mind.

The tourist court cabin looked clean, the bed comfortable, but the walls were yellow from cigarette smoke. And she could smell Them–coloreds–even under the heavy layer of cleansers and detergents. Or was it merely the smell of guilt?

Marie sat on the edge of the mattress, blood pulsing in her feet. She found the silver flask in her handbag: brandy to help blot out the afternoon; brandy to help erase fleeting, jumbled memories; brandy to help her forget who she was.

An automobile puttered to a stop outside. Marie choked. *Too late.* A door slammed. Footsteps. A soft, polite knock. She reached for the door, and opened it.

His eyes sparkled emerald, dark and inviting, like an opulent bedchamber kept half in shadow–although his nose was crooked, although the blond, cropped hair accentuated the broadness of his cranium.

He kissed her on the cheek, but he wasn't real. He begged her to let him bathe. He'd driven for hours from Lafayette. He shaved with a straight razor. Water's too cold, he said. He tossed the razor on the mattress.

The sound of running water. A small watercolor hung crooked over the bed: a field of blurry yellow flowers. Marie's gaze wandered from the painting to the razor. She wondered how it would feel, the steel bruising her flesh, opening her up to the sweet bliss of forgetfulness. *If he touches me, he won't be real because I'm not real.*

Paper-thin minutes blurred into cardboard hours, compressed between four dingy walls.

I am not this woman.

* * *

In the early mornings, Zassy lay awake in bed, listening to the pulse of the world slowly awakening around her: sparrows chirping when the sun crowned the eastern horizon, melting across the pines and the perfumed dogwood with an orange glow; Frank's light breath in the crib across the room; the steady, sonorous wheeze from Jolene lying beside her; and the ghostly shuddering of the walls and floors of Bellwether itself, a house alive with memory.

This was what she wanted, this baby, this house. Wasn't it? Strange how the polished wood in the foyer and the deep cherry of the winding banisters looked the same as they had in her dreams, but they weren't really hers. And it wasn't Frank Senior lying beside her, rather a woman whom she'd once hated because she was supposed to. Yet somehow, Zassy felt content. Somehow, eager. And somehow, completely alone.

Teense had definite ideas about the cooking and cleaning. When Zassy scrubbed the floors she should never use circular strokes, she should buff gently back and forth, back and forth. When she folded the linen she would iron creases *into* the bedclothes and tablecloths, and when she washed, she would never use over one-third-cup starch. She would polish the appliances and the furniture in the same manner as the floors: back and forth, back and forth. And Teense told her that there were only certain people she should talk to when sent to town on errands.

Teense told Jolene how she wanted the food prepared:

"Never, never more than a pinch of salt in anything, and I do mean a pinch. Let me show you." She nipped a bit of salt from the crockery, held it up for Jolene to scrutinize, and let it sift between her fingers. "Some people think this is a pinch." She poked her hands into the salt again and nabbed a dash more. "I say, no ma'am. Too much salt ruins the food. When Samson comes home you'll have to know how to prepare the pot roast so it's just the right shade of pink on the inside, no more, no less. He likes four meals a day. A sausage and hotcakes breakfast, two lunches, one hot, one cold, one at noon, the other at four, and dinner, which is always the biggest meal, at eight. Samson likes his potatoes fried, not baked, he likes his rice a little stiffer than the rest of us, he likes . . . ."

And Jolene would nod and say Yes'm and No, Ma'am.

However, even with all the preparations for Samson's return, Zassy, Jolene and Teense still had time for Frank.

"I wish Marie would come down from her room and play with this baby," Teense said, bouncing him lightly in the crook of her arm. "I know he'd cheer her up."

"She's always so sad," Zassy remarked.

"She misses Samson," Teense replied. But the woman's round, pinched face betrayed another worry. "We've got to get her out of that room," she said.

"What do you think's wrong with her?" Jolene asked as she readied for bed.

"I don't know," Zassy said. "I can't figure her out. But I don't think it's her man she's pinin for." She laid Frank in the crib, his eyes already closed. "I've gone up every time Miss Teense wants me to, and I knock and knock and don't get no answer. Except once I hear her say go away. Sound like she's whisperin on the other side of the door, pressed right up against it."

Zassy pulled her dress over her head and smoothed the shift over her pronounced curves, breasts round and full with milk. "Miss Teense said she's worried Miss Marie's sittin up there drinkin all the time. Said she's worried people'll start talkin and it won't look good for Mister Samson." She stretched out on the mattress beside Jolene and turned off the lamp. "What do you think's wrong with her?"

"Don't know," Jolene said. "But what about you, Hon? How you doin?" She stroked the curls away from Zassy's forehead.

"I'm all right." She wanted to say *I miss Frank*, but caught herself. *No. Time to move on, ain't it? Time to grow up and stop wishin for things that ain't gonna happen.*

Jolene caressed Zassy's smooth shoulder with a tentative touch, brushed the curve of her bosom, her midriff, and rested a hand on Zassy's hip.

But Zassy's hand fell atop Jolene's.

"Jolene," she whispered. "Don't."

Teense knocked softly. For the third night in a row, Marie didn't answer, so Teense padded back down the hall to her own room, unsettled–about Marie, and that baby. About the pull he had over her: the need to know he was near, the feeling of being incomplete when he wasn't.

The bedside lamp illuminated a massive oaken headboard, a patchwork quilt, great bedposts, and Daddy's sword, mounted on the wall behind it. Colonel Jean Boudreaux had died on that sword–his own–wielded against him by a Yankee at Manassas. When those pale-faced, tattered men presented the weapon to Mama, she'd cried, said she didn't want it. But Teense did, because even though it represented his death, it also brought him closer to her.

At fifteen, she'd rescued her father's photography equipment from the attic where her mother had put it away. The heavy wooden boxes and fragile lenses, flash powders and plates, were practically new since Jean never really had the chance to use them before. How Mama begged her to leave it alone. But Teense wouldn't be deterred. Because with his camera, she might find him again–in death, in the faces of the deceased. Like the faces of her younger brother, John, and his wife, Julie, dead of yellow fever so young, leaving Teense to care for their only child, Samson.

In recent years, she searched the papers for the

obituaries of complete strangers and their places of interment. It was less threatening and anonymous when she set up her cameras in funeral homes without the presence of the families. Most mourners didn't relate to her artistic endeavors, but Teense knew what she was after: real truth, the ugly, vulgar truth. Only in death can any of us find it.

However, it was not only physical death she felt compelled to photograph, there were baptisms to record, too: deaths of the soul, rebirths into consciousness and love. She recorded the moment for eternity, and if anyone wanted a copy, she'd be glad to make them one for a dime.

But tonight. Tonight when she held that baby, the air around him so . . . thick. And had she actually felt warm waves lapping at her ankles, cleansing as a baptism?

"Good night, Daddy." Teense kissed her fingers, raised them to the wall over the bed, then switched off the lamp.

And felt a shudder pass through the belly of the world.

The days grew longer, the sun angrier, the women of Bellwether lost in a vast sea of empty rooms: long hallways yawning like mouths ready to swallow, despair seemingly seeping from the walls like dewy tears.

Zassy grew cool toward Jolene. She attached herself to Teense, followed the little woman from room to room, eager to immerse herself in Teense's every whim–and Teense never tired of giving orders.

Zassy wondered if the humiliation showed in her face, that she'd let another woman touch her. Shamefaced and flushed, opening herself to those sweet caresses so much more tender than Frank's. She asked Teense where she might find a church, and if she could attend. Teense told her about a colored church just across the bridge in Westlake, and the next Sunday, Zassy bundled Frank and covered the three miles on foot.

Teense couldn't bring herself to tell Zassy about the feelings that overpowered her when she held Frank. Couldn't tell her that the emotions he stirred in her were of such force that she sometimes literally shook. Couldn't tell her about being afraid of the child because she was so drawn to him, or not to take Frank away because she needed him near. A single stroke of his cheek and she was good as new, revitalized. He was a crutch for her insecurities. Some people took to drink, others to God. For Teense, the child was both: intoxication in his very presence.

Jolene grew edgy, careful of her actions around Zassy. Sorry for her transgression, she wallowed in the guilt of having taken advantage of her. She stood polite and soft-spoken, did everything Zassy asked her to.

In June, the newspapers reported the United States Fourth Marine Brigade made a strong assault in the Belleau Wood on the road to Paris. Eight thousand confirmed dead. And Samson?

Teense threw herself into homecoming preparations with more fervor. Of course Samson would come home. Just because Marie hadn't received a letter from him since before the strike, didn't mean what they feared most was true. Just because no communication came from the front lines anymore didn't mean he would never come back.

So curtains needed washing and windows needed cleaning and someone needed hiring to help Silas with the yard work. Teense finally settled on a toothsome colored boy named Andy to help care for the grounds.

While upstairs, a woman came to know a stranger living within her:

"Who are you?"

Don't you know?

"No."

I'm Marie Boudreaux.

"How can you be? I'm Marie Boudreaux."

So am I, but I'm the one who's quit carin whether she lives or dies, and I'm winnin. I'm the one who's content to waste away and to forget. Because it's better that way, to forget. Forget Samson. He doesn't love you. He never has. And don't bother wonderin whether you should run away. You know you'd never make it without his money. You know you're not cut from the cloth to succeed without a man. You're an uneducated woman whom everyone else knows what's best for. You have nothin to say, so keep your mouth shut. No one cares what you think. No one cares about you except the brandy. It's tryin to help you by blottin out all those thoughts gettin jumbled in your head, all those things that confuse you and make you angry. Let it help you. It only wants to help you feel nothin so you can get on with things, so you can wander through your days not knowin or carin, not thinkin or feelin. And when you can't feel, you can't hurt anymore, Marie. Remember how peaceful Mama was in her last days? Remember Doc Barr sayin a little whiskey would do her a world of good? You're just like her, aren't you? So afraid after your daddy shot himself over those bad investments.

"You're tryin to destroy me."

No honey, I'm only tryin to help. Let me be the strong one. Let me take care of us both. The devil's already reserved a room for us in Hell, and this is it. How does that bed make you feel, the very sight of it? Remember all those sticky nights there trapped under a man who didn't love you, who only wanted to use your body to perpetuate himself? And don't you remember he never once told you he loved you? Why should you care about a man like him? Go on. Let him take care of you. Take his granddaddy's money. He's so proud the family made it off the slave trade. Live in his home. That'll teach him, won't it? That's the best revenge, livin off a man who can't stand you. So why not make the days as easy on yourself as you can, honey? Why not take a little more brandy to calm your nerves, huh? How about it?

This summer would never end.

* * *

Yet it did.

The regrets, unspoken recriminations, the fear and loneliness of being perched on a world ready to explode, drew to a close.

Deep into the dog days of August, a letter arrived from the United States Marine Corps addressed to Marie. Penned in an unfamiliar scrawl, it shook in Teense's hands, but she couldn't bring herself to take it up. Bad news? A regretful note? She carried it with her for two days unopened. If she left the envelope sealed, all those bad things she dreaded wouldn't get out, wouldn't see the light of day. If she didn't open the letter, Samson was alive.

But after fitful nights without sleep, when no prayer could alleviate the dread, she tiptoed down the hallway and slipped it under Marie's bedroom door.

Marie came out of her room the next afternoon, and halfway down the stairs. Teense, Zassy and Jolene greeted her with smiles, expectant and afflicted.

"He's wounded," Marie said. Her hair hung in clumps around a strained, pale face, the blood long drained away. "He's comin home."

The 11:05 from Baton Rouge ran late. Teense sat on a bench in the shade of the depot awning, stirring the air around her with a cardboard picture of Jesus stapled to a thin wooden handle: He stood in a green field surrounded by a flock of sheep. Teense wore a yellow cotton dress. Her matching slippers didn't quite reach the ground, swaying sluggishly back and forth an inch above the concrete as the world shimmered with thickening heat. Mounted on a tripod beside her, she'd draped her camera with a tablecloth.

Zassy sat a few feet away with Frank on the Coloreds Only bench. Teense insisted she accompany her and bring the baby. She let her get dressed up nice, too, in a plain white blouse tucked into a long black skirt.

Teense took a silver pocket watch from her bright yellow handbag. Although the watch was rusted, there was something akin to tempting fate about polishing it, like wiping away all evidence of a sure past to prepare for an uncertain future. 11:35.

The shock of a high-pitched whistle startled her with its proximity. A massive beast of iron and steel ate away at the tracks, plumes of hot white steam billowing from above and below. Teense and Zassy came to their feet. Teense squinted through the viewfinder.

An angry hot wind heralded the arrival. Mighty steel wheels squealed as the brakes took hold and the train slowed to a stop in a noisy knocking of metal against metal. Finally, the hiss of steam subsided. Two white women came from inside the depot and stood a few feet away. The doors opened with a metallic grind. Teense peered up and down the length of cars. Then spotted him.

Samson wore civilian clothes, a duffel bag slung over his shoulder, a solid vision through the steam. Muddy brown hair grew in a short stubble on a scalp recently shaved clean, ice blue eyes and rigid posture betraying no evidence of war or emotion. He looked like he'd come from across town instead of half a world away. He wore a beige jacket, matching trousers, a narrow black tie twisted into a hasty bow at his throat.

"Samson!" Teense waved.

He brought thin lips into a smile, wide but not endearing. Maybe this was where the strain of war would show, not in his eyes or the lines of his face, but the smile, the translator of the heart. He moved off the bottom step and shuffled along the concrete at a brisk yet pained pace. He drug his right leg.

"Stay!" Teense called. "Stay!" She uncovered the camera and framed him in her sights.

He stopped, a glimmer of humor at his eyes and lips eating away the straight lines of his face.

"Now smile real big for your Ain't Teensy, hear? Ready? One . . ."

He laughed, life stirring in his shocking blue eyes.

" . . . two . . ."

His gaze landed on Zassy and the baby. A noticeable cloud came over his face, somber and black.

". . . three! Got it."

Finally, he limped toward her, dropped the duffel bag onto the concrete, and bent low to wrap long arms around his aunt.

"Does it hurt very much?" Teense murmured under her breath. "Where did–?"

"Hip," he said. "It's nothin." He raised his gaze to peer over Teense's shoulder.

"You gonna keep your head shaved like that?"

Samson looked back. "I had it all grown out for a while."

"What happened?"

He looked back over her shoulder at Zassy and Frank. "Lice," he said.

"You poor thing. And you always had such a pretty head of hair. Well, it'll grow out again. Looks like it's on its way."

"Where's Marie?"

Teense lowered her gaze to her yellow slippers. "She's not . . . well."

"What's wrong?"

"She's just lonesome, honey." She looked up again. "She's been missin you so much, that's all. She hasn't been the same since you went off to the war, afraid you'd never come back."

"Is that what she said?"

"You know how quiet she is. You could see it on her face, though. It showed."

"Has she been drinkin again?"

Frank began to cry in Zassy's arms, and Teense turned around.

"This is my new girl, Samson. Rosa ran off when her husband came back. There's another girl, too. She does the cookin."

"Two?"

"We really need two. There's so much to do. Rosa really couldn't do it all by herself."

"This other girl, she a nigger, too?"

"That's all right, isn't it? Rosa was colored."

"Don't matter." He lowered his gaze on Zassy and offered her a forced smile. "You know what I say, niggers got a place, too. They just need to be reminded, from time to time, where that place is. You got a name, girl?"

"Yessah," she replied softly. "Zassy Cole. This here's Frankie."

"Well hush him up. I can't stand a baby that squalls all the time."

"Yessah." She rocked him, but it didn't help.

"Well go on ahead of us if you can't shut him up. And take that." Samson pointed to his duffel bag.

Zassy gave him a wide berth and bent to lift the bag by its drawstrings. She hoisted it over her shoulder and balanced Frank in the crook of her other arm, the bag thumping the backs of her legs as she made her way to the depot door.

"Girl, what do you think you're doin?"

She stopped, turned. "Sir?"

"I don't see any sign says niggers welcome anywhere, do you?"

"No, sir."

"You go on around the corner there and we'll meet you

on the other side."

"Yessah." Zassy shuffled away.

"You didn't have to do that," Teense said. "She's a good girl. Always minds whatever I say. And that baby. He–"

"Hush up," Samson hissed. "I don't wanna hear it. Everybody knows you give niggers an inch and they take a mile."

The shadow of a man stood in her bedroom. She heard his breath, but he didn't speak. She shuddered as he floated to her side.

"Marie."

His voice wound from some subterranean depth. Sympathy washed his features, left him expressionless. His gaze wandered to her soiled nightgown. Disgust tinged the corners of his mouth. His eyes found the nightstand beside the bed, the empty glass. He wrinkled his nose, wrapped strong fingers around her fragile wrist, pulled her close enough to smell him: stale sweat and the hint of faded toilet water. Lilac?

"No," she whispered.

She crashed to the floor, pulled with brute force from the bed. She cried out. He drug her across the room. She kicked. He pulled her into the hallway along the polished floor. He shouted downstairs: something about water, something about a bath. She pleaded. He silenced her with a sharp slap to the cheek. A shrill buzz grew in her ears.

No, you can't feel it if you're not real.

"You disgust me," he barked over the high whine in her head. "You think I've come home for this? This filthy cunt of yours?"

* * *

Days rushed one into the next. The clouds of war began to abate over Europe and soon, no doubt, the men there would come home: leaders, fierce minds and determined souls to set the country straight. Too much neglect left the women foolish in thinking they could do a man's job.

Samson knew decision-making of all kinds was better left to those who knew best: white men. All anyone needed was a strong man to show them the way, as Samson himself staked his territory, prepared for the future. The days blazed with a crystal blue hope, and the women of Bellwether seemed caught in his orbit. The energy emanating from him was infectious, and what once seemed minute became of greatest importance.

The plantation wasn't clean enough, he said, it would never be clean enough. Zassy scrubbed all the harder, brought a gleam to the surface of the polished wood, poked into dingy corners and cleared away the cobwebs. She brought light into the darkest recesses and parted the shadows while Jolene cooked and failed and cooked and failed again. Samson left her in tears on two occasions when he refused the dinner and threw the plates at her feet.

"What the hell is this?" he said. "I told you it should never be undercooked. Are you tryin to poison us? Think you'll just start slow and kill a few whites at a time? Is that how you niggers think you're gonna take over?"

"Samson!" Teense's extra chin wobbled over a tight collar of black ruffles she'd worn in anticipation of dinner. "She's done so well for us before. Give her a chance, huh, sugar? She'll learn the way you like things. We've been over lots of things, but we haven't gotten around to all of them yet."

"The nigger learns to cook or she's gone. Understand, Teense?"

She nodded.

And Jolene was miserable.

Zassy stood rigid with attentiveness whenever Samson raged. After he'd gone, though, after the sting of his words had time to infect the air with their poison, she walked away and didn't speak. Her stoic demeanor said what her mouth wouldn't.

All the tension made the air tangible and it didn't take long for everyone to notice its quick dissipation. Most of it swirled around Samson and spent itself in his frantic discourses: he'd finish his law education soon, pay his dues, then run for a post in the City Cabinet. From there, on to the Parish, State; a methodical plot to realize a seat on the Legislature, and who knew where that might lead?

It was time he made people realize that the ideas Samson Boudreaux had were the universal ideals that all men should strive to emulate. He would show the populace that the tide of progress could go on as long as things remained much as they always had: the whites keeping to themselves and the coloreds in communities of their own. There was already enough presentiment in his world to help fan the flames of an old-fashioned platform, to drive a wedge conclusively between the races. No more mixing, that's what caused all the problems now. With segregation, each class of the world would succeed and prosper.

All this he planned and calculated and reasoned over hours in the study where he limped and paced among moldering volumes of law and lore: ancient leather bindings cracked, musty with the scent of age. He also realized he'd need a family to cement his position in the public eye, and this, too, was a methodical process–of entrapment–with the woman who wouldn't look in his face when he bucked atop her:

"You're gonna have a baby for us." His hips thrashed in a peculiar fashion. "And if you take a drink while you've got my baby inside you, I'll kill you. Understand, sweetheart?"

But Marie didn't reply.

Teense prayed.

Jolene cooked.

Zassy cleaned and scrubbed and devoted all her spare time to Frank, who grew bigger each day. There wasn't time to think of the past, to lose herself in memories. Everyone hurtled toward a future they weren't quite sure of. The world, it seemed, spun faster, and threw everyone off balance.

The war, at last, came to an end, yet in its wake an influenza epidemic swept through Boston, New York and Philadelphia. Millions dead? Things like worldwide epidemics never got beyond the walls of Bellwether.

On Christmas Day, Marie made the announcement: the future grew in her womb, gestated in the empty space where she'd so often found the oblivion of apathy. One day children would grow into their roles as adults, and the burdens of life would shift to their capable shoulders.

Thank God. In time they'll forget me.

Which is exactly what Marie hoped. And everyone was delighted for her.

Jolene sat beside Frank's crib sewing a new dress when he laughed aloud. She put the dress aside, picked him up, cradled him in her arms, and sang under her breath in a whispered wheeze. She'd put on fifteen more pounds with the lack of physical labor she'd become accustomed to, and what had once been muscle now turned to fat.

"Look at that crooked smile," she said.

He fingered the silver thimble on her thumb.

"You're a good baby, ain't ya, Frankie?" she said.

"Yes," he replied. Flecks of emerald flashed in his eyes.

Jolene held him at arm's length and stared, shock numbing to a strange acceptance. He started to squirm, so she laid him back in his crib and his face immediately grew pinched.

Dizziness descended in her stomach. She clutched tight the crib's wooden railing. Weak in the knees, her heart fluttered, her legs twitched with that alien sensation of flying.

And then her spirit raced for the ceiling, burst through the cracked plaster and the rotting timbers, toward a violent blue sky. Clouds invaded her eyes. She rose toward a warm light that enveloped her with the love of its glow. The shape of a man materialized, but the light remained so intense Jolene couldn't make out the face atop his frame. From that dense light burst an even more radiant ray of salvation: of acceptance and unconditional love. The beam from those eyes pierced her heart, overwhelmed her with joy in a hot, sweeping flood.

But her feet slipped from the clouds and she plummeted through a sky grown indigo with night. Her spirit crashed through the roof and plunged into the top of her head, smashed into her feet before settling back into the fit of her physical self. She rocked with the violence of it, gripped the side of the crib with all her might. Sounds from the baby came to her ears. She felt heartbroken to be back in this world, puzzled at Frank's odd squeals, and horrified to realize he choked.

She trembled, heard a bubbling cough as air whistled at the back of Frank's throat. He turned red. Then a deep plum, a sickening purple, emerged in his cheeks. Jolene pried his lips apart, poked her fingers in his mouth and found the thimble. Air swept into his lungs. The color of his face turned back through shades of crimson, and he cried harder. Jolene took him to her breast, rocked him, shushed him as the hammer of her heart tripped. But he howled even harder.

Zassy appeared, alarm in her voice and eyes.

"What's wrong?"

"He's all right. Just got choked."

Zassy took him away from Jolene and rocked him

against her breast. "What's he chokin on?"

"Don't know." Behind her back, Jolene slipped the thimble onto her thumb, hating herself for lying, but– "He's all right now."

Zassy shushed him, stroked his thick black hair.

"He talked, Zassy," Jolene said.

"He what?"

"He talked. He said yes. Just like that. I said, you're a good baby, ain't ya, and he laughed and said yes, plain as ya please."

"He can't talk yet. Babies don't start talkin 'til they're at least nine months."

"But he did."

Tired from crying so hard, Frank's sobs waned.

"Do you ever get a strange feelin when you're holdin him?" Jolene asked.

"What do you mean?"

"I don't know, just strange, like you could fly or somethin?"

"That's mighty odd, don't you think?" Zassy pursed her lips and lowered her brow.

"Don't you feel it?"

"No. I never felt nothin like that."

"You probably think I'm crazy, don't ya?" Jolene lowered her gaze to the floor.

"Well, not . . . crazy."

Jolene looked up. The hard line of Zassy's mouth had broken into a faint smile, and Jolene offered a meek grin in return.

Most everyone doted on the child, fussed after him, praised and encouraged him. Frank learned to crawl, then walk. His legs wobbled and shook like a spring foal. The child was the future: the hope for good, the denial there can ever be any evil in this world.

He needed new clothes often and Jolene would stitch and sew into the small hours. When Marie gave birth, there would be another baby, too, and the children would be bound to each other through familiarity, in a world where, black or white, no one knew the rules for the game of prejudice. Jolene felt the promise of the very young bridging a gap between the races, the sincerity of childhood. She prayed the children would someday give Samson comfort.

Zassy stood amazed at how fast Frank grew. One day she heard him speak, too. He said 'Mama', plain as you please. With his birth had come the weight of motherhood, yet it was joyous to do for him–her flesh, Frank's, together in his face, fighting for dominance: her eyes, his bone structure.

Nights, Teense took to her room and leafed persistently through her photo albums–because God was there, in the pictures of the dead and of the living. The dead were His will and the living were His love.

Marie watched the shattered reflection of sunlight through the vines outside her window. She breathed deep, past the baby squeezed inside her body grown tight and round. She watched the light dance and flicker, ebb and disappear, watched shadows grow long. And in them, she found comfort.

She'd had nothing to drink since December. Not that she hadn't thought of it. *Give him a defective child. Think of his humiliation.* She craved the bittersweet fire that emptied her of all pain and emotion, all thought, but from time to time she also thought about the child. It wasn't named yet, but it was human, and inside her. It *was* her. But it was him, too. Samson hadn't laid a finger on her since she'd announced her pregnancy–which she regarded as a blessing–although he glared at her as if she should be able to hurry the process along.

Samson paced and cursed and studied, talked on the

telephone from seven in the morning until well after midnight. Some days he ventured into Lake Charles or Westlake. Twice, he made trips to Baton Rouge in hopes of lobbying for funds to finance a campaign. After all, wasn't the Congressional Majority Republican like himself?

He extolled the virtue of the Time–for him, for all men. The time to take advantage of a new life, a post-war economy, to grab opportunity by the kite-strings before it simply flew away. This was the time all common men waited for: to succeed, to win, to rule. And Samson Boudreaux would lead the way. But even with Boudreaux money and Boudreaux ideas, he needed Boudreaux constituents, too, because there wasn't as much of that Boudreaux money as there had been in the past.

He sold off fifty acres of Bellwether and became so angry when the buyer discovered a sulfur mine that he remained unapproachable for days. The metallic hum of progress floated from the pit some fifteen hundred yards away and rose into a cacophony of financial despair. Each gaseous sigh from the hot water drilled into its veins, each bite into the earth tempered his anger.

Some nights, he ventured toward the site, where the trees thinned and a gradual plane sloped toward the edge of the pit. There, the earth fell away in formless chunks, and below, crusty, bone-colored stalagmites splintered toward the sky. Sometimes enraged tears seeped from Samson's eyes, coupled with the sting of sulfur dioxide on the air.

And sometimes, he didn't come home at all.

He awoke to the hazy image of an unfamiliar room, eyelids like sandpaper, mouth glued tight. Consciousness brought the onslaught of a driving rhythm in his head, of a stink that penetrated to the point of nausea. He groaned, brought his hands to his face, found small beads of perspiration on his forehead.

The insistent buzz of a horse fly caught his attention. He followed its schizophrenic path toward an open window, where yellowed lace curtains danced on a quick breeze, a momentary reprieve from the humidity. Dark clouds festered on a gray morning horizon. Lightning flashed. Thunder rumbled with the promise of rain.

"Wattizit?" The girl rustled beside him.

"Gonna rain," he replied.

"I love zee rain." The ebony-skinned youth stretched her arms over her head.

Lightning flashed again. Thunder invaded the room. He pulled himself from the bed and reached for his shirt and trousers.

"Wattizit?"

"Nothin."

"You go?" She sat up, naked.

"Got to before it starts rainin."

"You come see me again?"

"Sure." He pulled on his shoes.

"You keess me good-bye?" She smiled, reclined on her arms, and spread her legs, ready to devour him with forbidden delights again, ready to punish him. Only in the darkest of skin could a man find the ultimate degradation: the feverish sublimation to a world shuddering out of control. He remembered the smell of her sex: unclean, yet tantalizing, like overripe plums. He turned to the door.

"You pay me now."

He stopped, dug the remaining bills from his wallet, and placed them on the banana crate beside the bed.

"You come again tonight?" She smiled.

But he pulled the door closed behind him. Thunder. The thunder called Samson outside.

He drove the inconspicuous sedan in rain through Westlake, overwhelmed with the need to bathe, to wash away the humiliation, that warm, moist itch. Closed markets, hardware shops and fashion boutiques fell behind, but ahead, he saw the lights of a diner. He wanted coffee, and cursed himself when he realized he'd given all his money to the girl.

But Jimmy Hazard's mottled brown pickup puttered to a stop in front of the diner, and Samson pulled in beside him. Jimmy glanced over his shoulder, his lazy eye trembling in the left socket, the eye that kept him out of the service. He always looked like he was either just coming awake or falling asleep. Samson came onto the walk beside him, lifted his right leg with relatively little stiffness. Both men thrust their hands deep into their pockets.

"Buy me a cup of coffee, Jim," Samson said.

"Sure," Jimmy replied, and they walked inside.

Past several empty booths, Jimmy caught a swiveling barstool under him. Samson sat beside him, squinting against the glare in his blood-cracked eyes. Jimmy already smelled of oil and gas, and the day was only just started.

"Mornin, boys." Eva Shaw came out of the kitchen with a pot of coffee. She wore a baby-blue uniform, blonde hair swept up under a matching cap. Her cheeks gleamed from the greasy air. She turned over the mug in front of Jimmy and filled his cup.

"Mornin," Jimmy said.

Thunder rumbled low outside.

"Coffee?" she asked Samson.

"You got chicory?"

She nodded. "You be wantin a menu?"

He shook his head.

"Right back." Eva disappeared into the kitchen. Forty years old? Fifty? Whatever her age, it appeared she'd kept her figure. She returned a moment later and filled Samson's mug with heavy chicory.

"Thanks," he said.

"You bet." She winked. "Jimmy, you're comin right

up." Again, she disappeared.

Samson sipped his coffee. "You read in the paper the other day about them riots in Chicago and Atlanta?"

"Nope," Jimmy said, his gaze at odds with Samson's.

"Bunch of niggers protestin that picture show about the War and the Klan," Samson said.

Jimmy didn't reply.

Eva sat a plate of steak and eggs in front of Jimmy as the front door opened and two older men came in, along with the sound of rain.

"Mornin, boys."

The men greeted Eva and found a booth as she darted around the counter, coffee in hand.

Jimmy cut the steak and broke the warm yellow yolks, forked it all up in great mouthfuls. Samson sipped at his coffee. Jimmy wiped his mouth, lowered his voice:

"You know the Taylors who own the old Duval place?"

"They're lumber people, yeah?"

"Yeah."

Thunder grumbled outside.

"Friday," Jimmy said.

"Well, if it ain't my two favorite ladies!" Samson stood in the dining room doorway.

Teense startled over the newspaper's obituary section she'd spread on the table, raised a pudgy hand to her throat, then laughed. "Samson Boudreaux," she admonished. "Don't you be sneakin up on the girls like that. You scared the life right out of us." She fanned her flushed face with a limp wrist.

Samson turned his attention down table, where Marie looked out the high windows to a warm world smothered in rich shades of green. The sunlight nestled in her hair, glowing gold. Soft again, ephemeral in the radiance of motherhood.

But the muffled din of heavy machinery permeated the room, too: a low, hateful echo from that god-awful sulfur mine. Every day it seemed to grow louder and louder.

Marie turned to look at Samson and the light around her faded, sucked into the vast blue whirlpools of her lifeless eyes. She used up his life. All the energy he could expend, she could devour. She consumed all life around her, digested it, and spat it back out, drained and useless. He despised her for it. Familiarity and contempt had long ago dissipated into knowing and apathy. Yet his lean smile never faltered.

"Someone's sure been in high spirits lately," Teense clucked.

Samson thrust his hands into the pockets of his gray trousers and rose on the balls of his feet. "Well, why not, Ain't Teensy? I got every reason to be happy. Now that the goddamn war is over and people are gettin on with their lives, everybody's happier. I'll be a daddy soon and come August I've decided it's back to the books."

"You mean you're goin back to school?" Teense whined. "Already? With the baby comin? I thought you were gonna wait 'til next year."

"I have to. I've only got two more semesters before I take the bar."

"You're movin so fast though, honey. Don't you think you're goin too fast?"

Samson moved into the dining room, limp pronounced, then stopped and turned back to Teense, rage coloring his cheeks. His voice grew low and steady. "It hurts me to think you don't believe I can do this."

"We–We're all happy about school," Teense said, taken aback at his transformation. "It's just you've not been back long and we're gonna miss you all over again."

"That's not it at all!" A hard blue vein throbbed dead center in Samson's forehead, his face flushed with a sheen of angry heat. "You don't believe I'm capable of achievin what I've set out to do!"

"I always–I always knew you would," Teense stammered. "We've got to have somebody take hold of things. Why, I was just readin in the paper about one of those poor colored boys bein branded. Just like cattle. And you know what the lead story in the paper was? President Wilson bein awarded the Peace Prize. It doesn't make any sense, does it? I mean, how can there even be such a thing as a prize when we don't even have peace?"

But Samson didn't answer. He left the room and grimaced. The pain in the hip grew worse when his ire was up.

Summer in Louisiana grew unbearable, and with it, Zassy. She missed her mother. She told Jolene she wanted to go back for a visit, but couldn't bring herself to. What if Annabella had nothing to do with her, with her grandchild? Why had she never returned her letter? Zassy felt miserable.

No other man in Lake Charles caught her eye, nor at the New Covenant Church in Westlake, where she convinced Jolene to attend as well. She'd loved Frank, given him everything she had, every waking thought and desire, every wish and hope and sorrow in her heart. And it left her empty. She couldn't make the mistake of letting another man divert the emotions wound around the little boy she bounced on her knee and sang to and rocked to sleep. There would never be another man to take the place of her little man, because Frankie belonged to her, forever, no matter what. She told Jolene she didn't miss men at all.

In the night, while the baby slept, the sounds of the world grew vast and empty. Some nights, Zassy moved closer to Jolene, some nights, she moved away. But always she thanked God for her. She knew Jolene loved her and would always be there to take care of her, like God. She loved her for her strength at willing to carry on. She loved her for her familiarity to that other world where they came from. She loved her because it was the right thing to do.

Jolene had come to feel that Frank belonged to her, too. She could see where Zassy spoiled him, but she had little room to talk. Never had a child been so lucky, so loved. Never had there been a child more beautiful and perfect in every way.

Never had so much ridden on such tiny shoulders.

"But you'll turn Mister Samson around someday, won't ya, Frankie?" Jolene cooed.

To which he'd replied, "Yes."

And suddenly, there was God, living in her breast, warm and loving and filling her with hope.

During the hottest weeks of July, the inevitable introduction of sulfur came to the shallow well. The water had to be boiled and the air grew thick with the rotten stench. The washbasins and cooking pans collected a rust-colored grime. Zassy scrubbed harder to remove the stains that made Samson furious. He filed suit, but was thrust to the back of the docket, which enraged him all the more.

Teense vanished one afternoon after receiving a package in the mail. She veiled herself in black and never told anyone she'd sneaked down to the colored cemetery with her new box camera from New York City–so small she could take it anywhere–never let on to anyone that she didn't belong at the funeral.

She locked herself away that afternoon and developed the photographs, studied the chafe of rope that clung to the umber skin of the dead boy's neck, studied his young face, now so peaceful in eternal slumber. She scrutinized his mouth and the relaxed lines that appeared to have been so restless in life: always smiling or talking, kissing or praying, eating or laughing. But never again.

Behind his closed lids lay mirrored images of those

he'd loved, she knew. We don't go alone into the hereafter. We don't stand before God cut off from those whose souls we know on earth, do we? She hoped not. She didn't want to face God by herself: the omnipotent Being Whose eyes reflected the God of the Old Testament, ablaze with fire, and Whose smile belonged to the God of the New Testament, forgiving and kind.

The more pictures she took in search of answers, the more questions arose, thus the more pictures there were to take. The road to everlasting peace was filled with so many questions, and who better than the dead to try and tell us what the other side is like?

In Samson's dream, the day stretched long and cold, black and red. The sound of cannons came muffled from the distant gulf of another piece of time. Voices, too: faint, excited and horrified. But the real world for Samson, indeed the real world itself, was muck and mud, frigid and dark. The world was a dead-eyed boy, mouth agape, spitting up blood from the river flowing inside him. The world was a patchwork of infinitesimal instances all stuttering to become cohesive with the next.

And he woke. Shrapnel sang hot in his hip. The muted percussion of the mine echoed in his skull. Like the distant sounds of war. Like the war that raged inside him: the longing for peace, the need for adulation. He'd never be free of it. He pulled himself from bed and wiped sweat from his brow. Frozen in dream during the middle of the day, and still his body simmered in the tepid air.

He made his way downstairs and into the parlor where everything was as it should be: every line rigid, every angle tight. He limped to the dining room: every chair pushed against the polished mahogany table. Good. It pleased him. There wasn't room for clutter in Samson Boudreaux home.

The house seemed deserted. He was alone. And it felt wonderful. No one pushing against him. No one stinking up the air with their stupid words. No one begging for his attention. No one needed telling what to do.

But someone shuffled in his study. He opened the door and startled Zassy, a feather duster in her hands.

"Afternoon, Mister Samson."

No, he'd never truly be alone again. His spirit waned. He made his way to the desk, angry for allowing himself to be embarrassed by his walk in front of her.

"I'll finish right up and be out of your way," she said.

He sat, tapped a pencil, stared at her. Watched the shift of her buttocks under the pale gray skirt.

Then she turned, smiled, and said, "Is there anything else you need?"

He shook his head.

Later that evening, Samson happened onto a party in the kitchen for Zassy's birthday. She was fifteen. She sat at the small table where Jolene cut the cake. Teense bustled with her new camera.

"Evenin, Mister Samson," Zassy said with a smile.

He moved into the kitchen, propped an elbow atop a countertop. "I've been thinkin, Teense."

"What is it, honey?" Teense laughed, balancing Frank and the camera.

"I'm gonna be leavin soon," he said.

"Yes, honey."

Frank squealed.

"Will you put the goddamn nigger down, Teense?"

Silence.

Jolene took Frank from Teense and the little woman's fingers tightened on the camera.

"Like I said," Samson went on, "I've been thinkin. I'm

gonna need somebody to take care of my place in Baton Rouge when I go to school, and I thought . . . maybe the girl could do it."

"Zassy?"

He nodded.

"You mean take her with you?"

"Yes. The realtor said fifteen hundred square feet. That's too much for me to try and keep clean with school and all, and big enough so she'd have a room all her own."

"But what about–?"

"The other girl can take care of the baby and clean here."

"But–"

Samson raised a hand. "Now, no 'buts', Teense, I've thought this through."

"But Samson, I need Zassy here. You forget we have another baby comin? We can hire somebody to help in Baton Rouge. We could–"

"I want the girl. She does a decent job. And I'll be havin people in."

"What people?" Teense narrowed her eyes and thrust out her chins.

"What are you gettin so upset for, Teense?"

"You may be a lot of things around here, Samson Boudreaux, Mister Overseer. You may be a big man and used to gettin your own way, but you're not takin that girl with you. This is one time I'm puttin my foot down!" She stamped her foot and stared him in the eye, dared him.

"I'll go," Jolene said.

"There." Teense backed off and whispered under high, singsong breath. "You can take her."

"Forget it," Samson said, then limped to his study. Who the hell did she think she was, talking to him–Samson Boudreaux–that way? And in front of them. Well to hell with her. To hell with them, too. He cursed the darkened walls, slammed a fist on the desk, and bloodied a knuckle.

A blazing blue noon in August arrived when Samson said his good-byes and everyone wished him well. Teense watched from the verandah as the gleaming automobile pulled from the drive, Marie watched from her window upstairs, Zassy and Jolene peeked through the lace curtains in the parlor.

Teense came inside, climbed slowly upstairs, each movement calculated as if contemplating the consequences of the next step and the next. Then she vanished into the dim upstairs hallway.

"Well, he's gone," Jolene said.

But Zassy didn't hear her. She was remembering another hot day and another shiny black automobile and a tall, handsome man named Potter. For an instant, he was there, a glimmer from the ghostly patchwork of faded time. Then, like that sticky day in a crackling field under the watchful eye of God, the memory vanished.

And soon, all the sounds left in the house belonged to the faint repercussions of earth being eaten away in the distance.

Sunday: 1963

As Miss Zassy talked, the miles of I-90 fell away beneath the tires that carried us closer to Jennings. From there, we would go to Lafayette, then north toward Breaux Bridge, a region of rare beauty, and a country of nightmares, both real and imagined.

"See that gas station up there?" she said. "You mind stoppin?"

I pulled up to a pump and rang the service bell.

"Won't be a minute." Miss Zassy opened the door, stepped out, and disappeared around a mason-brick wall, carrying the plain brown package with her.

An attendant in thin gray coveralls came from inside, spat a brown stream of tobacco juice, and moved slowly toward the car.

"Fill it up," I said. "Premium."

He reached for the nozzle and I rummaged in the glove box to find new batteries for the recorder. Moments later, I saw Miss Zassy out of the corner of my eye.

"Nine dollars," the attendant said.

I counted ten and told him to keep it as Miss Zassy settled back beside me.

The attendant bent at the waist and peered in the window. "Where was you just now?" he asked her.

She didn't reply.

"Thanks." I rolled up the window and started the car.

"Was you usin the toilets?" His voice was muffled outside the glass, his ferret-like eyes narrow. "We don't have colored toilets."

But I slipped the car into drive and pulled back onto the highway.

After a moment of silence, I said, "I'm sorry."

"For what?" she asked. "For him? I don't never hear stuff like that no more, unless somebody points it out to me."

"Then I'm sorry for being sorry," I replied.

Miss Zassy turned her gaze out the window, to spring blooming into summer. "There's a lot of folks got reason to be sorrier than you," she said.

Part Two

Son

III

Her name was Alice. Blonde like her mother, she had the run of Bellwether. Whatever wish she had was always granted or greatly compensated for. She might have grown spoiled, but it wasn't in her nature. She never demanded or made unreasonable requests, she was kind and giving as the two colored women, now living in a reconverted quarter house on the property, taught her. Inadvertently, the women did a good deal of her rearing.

Marie stayed locked in her room all the time, gazing at a faded spot on the wall, where the sun had bleached the once delicate pink and yellow blossoms of the paper into a smoky-white haze.

Samson, however, spent long hours with Alice in his musty study, determined she should know the proper etiquette in dealing with all people. After he came to the Legislature in 1926, important people were always visiting Bellwether: congressmen and their wives, friends from Baton Rouge, where Samson spent three to four months of the year. But clients still met him at his office, Boudreaux and Lermontant, on Pine Avenue in Lake Charles.

About coloreds, Alice learned that the race was an inherently bad lot, that she should do her best to avoid them, to treat the women and Frank differently than she treated whites. She shouldn't treat them badly, only behave with an air of superiority, lest they think they could control her.

Teense had a debilitating stroke in the summer of 1928. Her pleasantly round face grew twisted, the left side draped in dead, fleshy folds. This wasn't Teense at all. But neither had she seemed the sort of woman to collect all those horrible pictures, either.

Young Alice stumbled across a photo album one day, and inside she found faces–dead faces–lined up one after another. Horrified, yet unable to stop looking, she dreamt about the faces that very night and woke screaming. Daddy rocked her back to sleep. The next day, she heard him cursing Teense, using words she should never utter, screaming about Teense being sick in the head.

And that afternoon, Teense raised a trembling hand and pulled Alice to the bedside, the dead half of her face monstrous.

"There's nothin to be scared of, Alice," she said, words clogged around muscles that wouldn't work anymore. "The people you saw in those pictures are those who are livin with God. They're the happiest people in the world, because they're at peace. Do you understand, honey?"

Alice shook her head.

"When we die, we go to God if we've been good on earth. If we've been bad, we go to the devil."

"How do you know all those people in the book are with God?" Alice whispered.

But Aunt Teense couldn't answer that question.

She asked her mother about God and dying, but Marie could barely talk, let alone try and explain. Her daddy didn't help, either. He said when you died you went to heaven, that's that.

"Where's heaven?" she asked.

"Up there." He pointed to the sky.

"Why?"

"Because there's no niggers there," he replied. Daddy said they went to another kind of heaven.

But Jolene had told her that the Bible said, 'Love one another'. So Alice wondered, *If Daddy hates coloreds, will he go to Hell?* He told her that whites and coloreds worshipped different gods, and that most coloreds worshipped the devil.

But surely not all coloreds, surely not Frank. He wasn't like the other boys, not like Ethan and Dooley Lermontant–her father's law partner's boys–who ran up and down the stairs of Bellwether while the men had their heads together in the study. Samson always ended up throwing them out of the house, where they never failed getting into worse trouble. Once, Ethan broke his leg at the old mine that dried up in '29; once, both boys got lost in the dense wood cropping off the property's eastern boundary, and were hunted for hours. When found near the river, they'd received the whippings of their young lives. Their father, Claude, made them choose their own switches. Dooley snagged an old limb, he'd learned this lesson already, but Ethan chose one young and green, and it stripped him of the soft skin at the back of his legs.

Ethan was a year older than Alice, Dooley three years her senior, and it was them that her father insisted she play with when she'd rather play with Frank; it was first Dooley then Ethan that Samson nurtured relationships with concerning Alice. Someday, he hoped the houses of Boudreaux and Lermontant might be one. Besides, he hated seeing her with Frank. The boy was sharp beyond his years, and Samson couldn't admit that coloreds had minds for anything other than hard physical labor.

At sixteen, Alice Boudreaux was one of the prettiest girls in Calcasieu Parish. She inherited her hair from her mother, but her blue eyes from her father; even at an early age they danced with a determination unseen in most children. She carried herself with a dignity uncommon but for those raised in the South: proud and self-sufficient. And her skin rarely ever saw the rays of the hot Louisiana sun. Only when shadows grew long under the towering pines and oak draped with Spanish moss, did she bare her shoulders and neck. Hers was a privileged life. She lacked nothing.

She floated through the kitchen and talked with Jolene, or gossiped on the phone in the parlor with girlfriends or a new beau. She held seats on the Student Council and Honor Society, was a member of the Debate Club.

Pleased she'd inherited his articulation, Samson was nonetheless guarded that she–a girl–should be so outspoken. She frustrated him, yet he envied her youth and enthusiasm. If it weren't for her, he'd have felt entombed along with the other women on the second floor.

Marie's once striking features had eroded under a plump layer of skin, flesh the look and consistency of Jolene's drop-biscuit dough. Gone, the life from her eyes and mouth; gone, too, any evidence of whom she'd ever been. Only Zassy or Jolene or Alice ever entered her room, everyone whispering under their breath as if the slightest noise would shatter her like a porcelain doll. And the room smelled. Because Marie was literally pickling in the alcohol, putrefying in the heat.

Teense's room smelled, too. Even though the women gave her a bath every other day and changed her bedding and gown, she stank of decaying flesh. Slipping fast. Doc Hadley, the only GP in town who wasn't a quack in Samson's opinion, told him that it was only a matter of months for her. And since Samson knew that what sets a gentleman apart from the rest is his ability never to admit when anything is wrong, the women on the second floor died a little more every day, but few took notice.

* * *

Jolene told Frank he reminded her of his daddy, but about the man, Zassy never spoke.

"Did he die?" young Frank questioned.

Jolene shook her head. "Maybe someday your mama will tell ya. That's best left up to her, I guess."

The only Father he knew lived in Heaven.

At eight years of age, Frank came to Brother Preston, the sleepy-eyed, silver-haired Pastor of the New Covenant Church. Preston leaned across the desk and took Frank's hands, warm and very much alive in his own. "What questions do you have, son?" he asked.

To which Frank replied, "I wanna see God. How do I know He's real? I know He lives in my heart, people tell me that's where He is, but I wanna see Him."

Preston smiled. A river of pure joy seemed to flow from the boy's hands and flood him with the warm waters of salvation. "We have to have faith, son. That's all we have." The river flowed deep inside him.

"Miss Teense," Frank continued. "Alice showed me bad pictures."

"What pictures?"

"Dead pictures. Miss Alice said they were happy because they were with God, but I don't know. They don't look very happy to me."

So they prayed, and in the days and nights to come, there would be many more times spent on bended knee, palms pressed together, eyes closed. Preston stood in awe of the love and conviction he saw in Frank's face, gripped in the power of prayer, but sometimes shuddered at the placid transformation of the boy's features, reminding him so of the sweet face of Jesus.

Preston schooled Frank in the afternoons, and as the boy grew, so did his appreciation for the history and the math and the English. Fervent in his energy for the church, Frank finished up his chores at Bellwether each day, then cut the grass at the church or trimmed the hedges. He was first to pick up a brush at a paint fellowship, and devoted every spare moment.

He remodeled the old quarter house where they lived, from the smooth-sanded furniture to the cabinets with Bellwether's cast-off china, to the teak paneling and plaster. He refurbished the floors, and they gleamed under his mother's care. Solid and neat, the house possessed an air rich in familial comfort.

Frank grew tall, his body hard from working the grounds. He took over the upkeep entirely when he turned fourteen. His skin remained the color and texture of polished mahogany, smooth and brown, but his jaw began to hint at a beard, and his hair grew straighter rather than curlier, flowing in pronounced waves over the crown of his head. His favorite book was the Bible, from which he could quote verse after verse. At times, even Alice listened. It was the best way he knew to breach their worlds, with the power of Gospel. Yet he learned never to brush against a white woman, even on the sidewalk. He learned it was better to leave the walk altogether than risk the chance of accidentally touching her.

Jolene dressed Frank impeccably, and when he passed through a room, mothers nudged their daughters, women, young and old, flocked to him. But however tempted by the girls' inviting smiles, Frank remained steadfast and chaste. There was much learning to do first.

Brother Preston passed away in the spring of 1934, and Frank composed a eulogy for the funeral. When he finished, he'd mesmerized the mourners with hope and love, and ever afterward, the men would chide him, 'When you gonna take up preachin, brother'? And the women would fuss at him and say, 'But honey! You got the gift'!

Frank said he'd never considered the idea of taking up the Gospel. He was still a young man with many avenues to pursue. But he would never lose his love for the Lord.

And everyone believed him.

The moon shimmered over the river. The warm, black waters of the Calcasieu lapped against its banks in the darkness.

"Alice?" Frank said.

"What?" She moved closer beside him on the toppled pine, her feet skimming the water.

"Mama got a letter the other day."

"From who?"

"My . . . grandma."

"Grandmother? You've never said anything about–"

"No. I haven't. Because I never knew. Aunt Joe said her and Mama never got along, but the letter said my grandma was gettin old and wantin to put things right between 'em."

"That's sad." Alice placed a hand on Frank's shoulder and propped her chin on top of it.

"Mama didn't wanna go at first," Frank said. "But Aunt Joe convinced her it was the right thing to do. Mama wants me to go with her, but . . . ."

"But you don't want to," she finished for him.

He lowered his head.

"Everybody has doubts," Alice said. "You wouldn't be human if you didn't."

"I know," he murmured.

Samson made phone calls in his study, drumming up donors for an upcoming charity dinner:

"Charlie Watson, old man! Samson Boudreaux!"

"Boudreaux? . . . . Yes, yes. Glad to come."

"Colonel Reese! Samson Boudreaux!"

"Boudreaux! . . . . Yes, fine, son. Be happy to stir up a little enthusiasm in the Rapides."

"Jefferson?"

"Jefferson Davis Montgomery, who's this?"

And the afternoon dissipated in renewed acquaintances, and helped bolster Samson's chances for bid come election.

"What say you this here orphanage?"

"Saint Tammany, Admiral. Sad state she's in, yes, sir."

"Why, that's a mighty fine cause you got yourself there, boy. Ain't that Cath'lic affiliated?"

"Yes, sir."

"You ain't Cath'lic. What you gettin out of it?"

"Admiral?"

"You hear me, boy. The Church is just as corrupt as any other party. Always has been. You're not thinkin on little kickbacks here and there? A little personal relations, maybe?"

"Sir. I beg to differ."

Samson slammed down the phone, swiveled his chair, and glared out into the night, to the patchwork of light thrown from his study window onto the lawn. He spotted Alice and Frank walking up from the river.

Zassy tried to convince him that afternoon to let her and Frank go to Alexandria, but Samson refused. He said he'd had to hire extra help as it was for the one hundred dollars a plate affair, and he couldn't afford to let her go, what with all the preparations. But now, Samson raged.

To hell with it. Let 'em go. Get him away from her. People can be hired. Hell, people can be bought.

He sent for Zassy, but at sight of her smooth, dark skin, he swallowed, then cleared his throat.

"I've changed my mind. You two go on. But Jolene stays."

"Thank you, sir." Zassy lowered her gaze and an anxious smile trembled at her lips.

"Don't you go thinkin you can just take off any time you want from now on. You've still got a job to do here, woman."

"No, sir." Zassy shook her head. "Yes, sir." She nodded, raised her gaze back to Samson's.

"You go on now and tell Alice I want her inside."

"Yes, sir. And thank you again, Mister Samson." She turned, left the study.

And Samson choked. Jesus and God. It had been a long time since he'd had a woman. Because everyone would know. Everyone saw him with the cane. Everyone knew the sound it made along the tiled hallways of Boudreaux and Lermontant. 'Mornin, Mister Boudreaux!' the painted dolls called before he even entered the room. What young beauties they were, the typing pool. They wore their merit on their fuzzy pink sweaters and tightly belted waists. Tasty as strawberry jam, tart and ripe. Yet, there was nothing quite like the flavor of dark molasses melting on hot buttered biscuits.

He picked up the phone and dialed.

"Oh, yes, sir. It's gonna be a real affair. Be most anxious for y'all to come on down to Lake Charles."

The train slowed as it approached the Alexandria station. Frank peered out the window, his reflection opaque on the glass: the black waves of his hair slicked back, a long black tie, a snowy-white, short-sleeved shirt. Beside him in the colored coach, Zassy stared straight ahead at the backs of the other three passengers. She wore a small black hat, a pale yellow blouse and gray skirt, nylons, and an old pair of black flats polished to a shine. Mother and son had spoken little since they'd boarded.

Once stopped, Frank gathered the two scuffed suitcases, and he and Zassy disembarked from the rear, intending to cover the distance to his grandmother's on foot. But a thick, meek voice came from behind.

"Miss Zassy?"

A large black man with doddering eyes and silvered hair, wearing tan trousers and a plaid shirt, rolled and unrolled the limp brim of a hat in nervous, oversized hands.

"Luther?" Zassy said.

"That's me, Miss Zassy." He smiled.

"What you doin here?" She returned the smile and hugged him close.

"Your mama." Luther released his hold on her. "Done sent me to pick you up. Why, you's prettier than I remember."

"Luther." Zassy batted her eyelashes.

"This your boy?"

Zassy nodded and turned. "Frank, come say hello to Luther Spees."

Frank dropped the suitcases and offered Luther an outstretched hand. "How do you do."

"How do you do." Luther pumped Frank's palm. "Looks like your mama give you a proper raisin."

"Yes, sir."

"How's Ruth?" Zassy asked.

"Ruth's–" A cloud passed over Luther's face. "Ruth done passed."

"I'm sorry," Zassy said. "When?"

"Be eight years come September."

"I'm so sorry, Luther." She paused for a moment, then asked, "You got kids?"

"Yes, ma'am." Luther's face brightened. "Two fine boys. Oldest boy done moved on and got married already."

"Grandkids?"

"Not yet. Before too long, though." He grinned from ear to ear. "Guess we better be gettin on, you two. Your mama, she'll be wantin to see ya."

* * *

"When'd all this happen?" Zassy asked.

Luther's bulbous gray Packard, scratches and dents along its battered hood, meandered past crumbling pine shanties as Frank peered out the window and listened from the back seat.

"All what?" Luther asked.

"All this."

"Just the sign of the times, I guess," he replied. "I know I do the best I can, but it still don't never seem to be enough. Farm me and you worked, bank foreclosed." He paused, then, said, "Almost home." He turned onto a dirt road.

Having seen so much decay, it was a relief to see well cared for quarter houses. The whitewashed wood needed a fresh coat of paint, but the walls looked solid, the porches swept, shaded by the large mimosa.

Frank saw a gray-haired woman standing on one of the porches, a white, crochet shawl draped across the shoulders of a drab gray dress. She stared at the automobile as it pulled to a stop, and at the trio climbing out.

"I guess that be my girl and her boy you got there," the woman called. "Well, bring 'em on in." She walked into the house and the screen door banged shut.

"Here we go." Zassy reached for Frank's hand and he followed her inside.

"Mama?" Zassy called.

"Here." Annabella's voice came from the kitchen.

Zassy moved across the room and hugged her mother. "I'm so glad to see you," she said.

"Me, too." Annabella didn't hug back, she merely patted at Zassy's yellow sleeves. "Me, too." She stood back and her gaze moved over her daughter in inspection.

"Mama, this is Frank." Zassy placed a hand on his shoulder as he joined them. "Kiss your grandma, Frank."

He kissed her cheek and hugged her.

But a strange look passed over her face and she pushed

him away. "Just have to get some air," Annabella said. "Gettin a little overcome, I guess."

"Here's your belongins." Luther set the scuffed suitcases on the floor.

"You stay for a piece of my blueberry pie, won't ya, Luther?" Annabella said, her voice tinged with desperation.

"Oh, no, ma'am. I'm gonna leave ya'll alone to get caught up." He turned to leave.

"Thank you, Luther," Zassy said.

"Thank you, Mister Spees," Frank echoed.

"Good-bye, Luther." Annabella's voice grew flat.

A moment later, the metallic thud of the car door came from outside and the engine revved.

"Let's sit down," Annabella said.

"How's Sister May?" Zassy asked, following her mother to the sofa.

"Married," Annabella replied, inching slowly into the cushions. "Met a nice boy and done had two kids of her own, boy and girl. Livin in Texarkana. My, that's a pretty hat."

"Thank ya." Zassy looked to Frank, still standing in the kitchen. "Come on, honey, sit down."

He obeyed and took a hard wooden chair beside the sofa.

"What's their names?" Zassy asked.

"Neely."

"I mean my niece's and nephew's."

"Ray Earl and Missy Ann."

"How old?"

"Four and two."

"How long they been livin there?"

"Five years."

An uneasy silence descended between them, weighing on the sunlight filtering through the window, dust motes glimmering like stars falling from a daylight sky. Frank slid a finger under his collar. Too tight.

"Frank, tell your grandma about your work for the church," Zassy said.

He looked at the old woman, but she wouldn't meet his gaze. Instead, she stared just over his shoulder.

"I-I don't know what you mean, Mama."

"Tell her about your schoolin with Brother Preston. Tell her about your Bible studies."

"What's to tell?" A web of sudden doubt ensnared him.

Zassy gave him a quick, imploring look before turning to Annabella. "Oh, Mama. Why, Frankie, he–he's just done made me right proud workin for the church the way he does. He gave the prettiest talk I ever did hear at a funeral last year. Why, he may even make a preacher someday."

"Like his daddy?"

"No, Mama."

"My daddy?"

"I hope not. You still with Jolene?"

"Yes, Mama."

"Well, I guess." Annabella let go a long sigh.

Frank's head spun. Dizzy. The air was too hot. Too thick. Too full. He closed his eyes. The women's voices faded. He willed away the nausea, opened his eyes, and saw four rectangles of sun cast from the window onto the dark wood floor. Elongated with late afternoon, the rectangles pulsed hot and white in the perfect pattern of a cross. Indefinable shame surged through Frank. Unexpected tears slid down his cheeks in warm, thin trails.

"I'm sorry, Mama," he said. "I don't feel well."

But Zassy looked stricken. She didn't speak.

Annabella gasped, eyes wide in horror.

"Mama?"

"Frank!" Zassy came quickly to his side. "What's happenin to you?"

"What do you mean?"

"Yea, though I walk through the Valley of the Shadow of Death," Annabella prayed, "I shall fear no evil."

"Look!"

Frank lowered his gaze, saw tears falling from his chin onto his snowy-white shirt.

And bursting in violent red explosions.

Doctor Reynolds washed his hands, then swiped at the nervous moisture on his brow. Zassy and Luther stood grim-faced in a corner of the examining room, Luther curling up the brim of his hat, smoothing it out, then curling it back up again.

"Is he all right?" Zassy asked.

"The bleedin has stopped," Reynolds said. "As far as I can see, he looks healthy in every other way. But . . . ."

"What?"

"It's . . . ." The doctor's gray eyes turned milky behind his wire-framed glasses. "Are you religious people?"

"We– Yes."

"So you're believers?"

"In what?"

Reynolds hesitated. "Stigmata," he muttered under his breath. He shook his balding head and said, "It's the only explanation I've got. The only one."

Zassy looked confused and upset.

"Blood of Christ," Reynolds explained. "Takin on the sufferin of the cross. Most cases, people's Catholic, but there's been some documentation in other religions, too. Although most I heard tell is it only happens durin Holy Week. Get wounds in their hands and feet like Jesus. Hold out your hands, boy."

Frank obeyed.

Reynolds took Frank's hands in his own, palms up. "Nothin here," he said. "What about your feet?"

Frank removed his shoes and socks.

"Nothin," Reynolds said. "How do you feel, boy?"

"Fine," Frank lied.

"I'm gonna send you on home then. You get some rest, and if it happens again you come quick as you can, hear?" Reynolds looked at everyone in turn.

Frank nodded.

"Yes, sir," Zassy said. "But Mama. She don't–want us comin back."

"You can stay with me," Luther said. "I'll take care of y'all."

But Zassy didn't reply.

"I'm sorry, Mama," Frank murmured.

Thirteen-year-old Tommy Spees couldn't shake the cold feeling he'd had ever since Frank had been put into his bed.

"What happened to him?" Tommy asked his father.

"He's just sick," Luther replied. "He just needs to rest for a day or two."

"What's wrong with him, ma'am?" Tommy asked Zassy. But all she said was that she needed to rest, too. She looked sad. The boy, he looked real sad.

Late in the afternoon, when everyone napped, Tommy sneaked a peek at Frank through a split in the wood of the warped bedroom door. He didn't want him there, and he didn't want to catch whatever he had.

At seven o'clock Zassy tried to feed Frank, but he said he wasn't hungry.

Then a knock came on the door. Luther answered. Young Miss Pauline, from a few doors down, stood on the porch. She said she'd heard what happened.

"What happened?" Tommy asked again.

"Hush," Luther said.

Miss Pauline asked if she could see the boy, but Luther said he didn't know. He called Zassy from the bedroom and introduced her.

"Miss Pauline, she's wantin to know if she can see your boy."

"Why?"

"It's a miracle!" Tears brimmed at Pauline's eyes. "Please let me see him. Please."

Zassy hesitated. "Well, I guess it'd be all right. He's in there." She led the young woman to the closed bedroom door. "Frank, honey," she called. "There's somebody here to see ya. To see how you're doin."

"Mama?" he asked before the women disappeared inside and the door closed again.

"He caused a miracle?" Tommy asked.

"Nope." Luther shook his head. "Miracle done happened *to* him, I guess."

And another knock came on the door.

Men and women asked to see him. The elderly asked to pray with him. The infirm asked to touch him. Overcome by self-consciousness, Frank grew angry. How could his mother allow this? He found peace only in an odd spiritual bliss descending on everyone's desperate faces. They believed him to be a channel for the blood of Jesus. His heart accepted, yet his head remained skeptical, filled with doubt.

And when they left, when Mama kissed him goodnight and turned down the light, Frank lay awake, wondering at what terrors God had in store for the man who questions.

Annabella sat in the dark and watched them come and go at Luther's. She knew what they said, why they congregated, but she wouldn't be party to it because it wasn't right. She'd felt it when she'd hugged her grandson, full of the same electric fire that burned around Mama Lena.

And the next morning when Zassy knocked, Annabella didn't answer.

Three days later on the train back to Lake Charles, Frank said, "Mama, tell me about my daddy."

So she did.

"I told you he was somethin special," Jolene said, lips twisted into a curious smile, eyes glassy. At first horrified with the story Zassy related to her, Jolene finally accepted it with a reverent understanding and secret joy: *This is the sign. This is proof I ain't crazy about all them feelins.*

Jolene took Zassy's chin in her hand and raised her head to meet her gaze. Eyes red, the strain weighed heavy on Zassy's features.

"I'm sorry about your mama," Jolene said. "But if she ain't willin to accept you and that boy, then it's her loss. She just don't understand, that's all. She's gettin older every day and more set in her ways. People do that. And they're just scared when they see somethin they can't explain."

"But–"

"You ain't never gonna change her and you might as well accept that. Just think of them other folks. Just think about them. Maybe your mama was never meant to love Frank, but look at all the other folks do."

Zassy lowered her gaze and turned away. "You're right." She sighed. "I only wish–"

"Now ain't you the one once said a girl shouldn't spend her time wishin about things?"

Zassy drew her mouth into a feeble smile. "You always know just what to say, don't ya?"

"Of course I do," Jolene replied. "Ain't that why ya stayed with me so long?"

Later that day, Jolene hugged Frank tight to her bosom, ready to embrace the heady waves she now understood to indeed be God's light.

"Please don't tell anybody," he pleaded.

Jolene pulled away, held him at arm's length. "Don't you understand what's goin on here? Don't you know you been touched by God? Ain't nothin to be ashamed of."

"But people'll–"

"People need to believe," Jolene said. "To believe in somethin more than themselves. People need faith. That's what keeps us goin. And when they're witness to a miracle, when folks see His power . . . ."

"What?"

Jolene shook her head and hugged him tight again. "It's a sign," she said. "He wants ya."

"I know." Frank pulled away. "But why me?"

"Who knows?" she replied. "The important thing is, you're His now."

That afternoon, Frank wielded a sickle against the encroaching vegetation when he noticed the shape of a man from the corner of his eye. He turned, saw a stranger standing in the road, wearing a tattered gray coat and dirty trousers bunched at the cuffs. Frank squinted against the glare of the sun, walked closer, and regarded the man's eyes. The walking dead seemed to stare at him from under the brim of a crumpled hat, yellow eyes splintered with red.

"Can I help you, sir?"

The man didn't move.

"Are you lost?" Frank moved closer, regarded the

olive, unshaven face: Mexican. "Do you speak English?"

"Por favor!" The man fell to his knees, grasped at Frank's hands and tried to kiss them. He started to sob, the lines of his face anguished, yet filled with a blind, terrifying love.

But Frank pulled away, dropped the sickle, and made a hasty retreat.

Two more Hispanic couples wandered up some time later, and at four o'clock, familiar black faces from the New Covenant Church appeared. But Frank wouldn't talk to them.

Everybody knows. But how?

So many despairing faces, so much curious hope in their eyes. Jolene said that news of miracles traveled fast, which induced in him a more profound dread. When would his spirit's desire to believe overcome the doubt of his human mind? When would it stop?

"What in hell's all them goddamn niggers doin down there?" Samson roared. And Miss Dandy Lee Ethridge, the hotshot society gal, due any minute to help make plans for the charity dinner. He shoved up a window in the study and yelled at the small group gathered near the drive: three women and two men. "Go on! Get the hell outta here!"

No one moved.

"I said go on! You want me to call the police?" Rage flushed his cheeks.

"We're here to see the boy!" came a man's upraised voice.

"What boy?"

"The boy been blessed!"

"What the hell are you talkin about?"

"Frank Potter!"

"What?"

"Hallelujah!" a woman cried. "Praise God!"

"Hallelujah!" Everyone raised their faces and hands to the heavens.

"Go on!" Samson yelled. "I'm warnin you! I'm callin the police right now!" He slammed the window shut and shuffled to the desk, the pressure building in his hip and his head. He swiped at the phone, but his finger was too shaky to dial, so he dropped the receiver, swaggered for his cane, and lurched into the hallway.

"Zassy!" he yelled.

"Mister Samson?" Jolene materialized from the kitchen, alarm in her voice.

"Where's that girl? Where's that boy?"

"She's upstairs, Mister Samson, sir. Takin care of Miss Teense."

"Get her! Get her and that boy!"

"Yessir." But Jolene only made it halfway to the staircase when Zassy appeared at the upper landing.

"Get down here!" Samson threw at her. "You!" He turned on Jolene again. "Get that boy! Now!"

Jolene disappeared back into the kitchen as Zassy came down the stairs and followed Samson into the parlor, ablaze with hazy red, late afternoon sun. He wheeled on the tip of the cane.

"You tell me what's goin on! Why all them niggers want to see your boy? What's he done?"

"I . . . ."

"Spit it out. Don't stand around wastin time like you usually do. What's goin on?"

"Frank," she said. "He's . . . been touched. By a miracle." Her voice grew bolder, although fear swam in her eyes. "He cried. Blood. Jesus' blood."

"Bullshit!"

"It's true, sir."

"I don't believe it." Samson pivoted on his cane and

walked stiffly to the window. He swiped the lace curtains back and saw the group still gathered at the end of the drive. Stopped several yards away, Miss Dandy Lee sat in her new white town car, unmoving. "Shit!" He brushed past Zassy and threw open the front door. "Go on!" he shouted from the verandah. "The police are on their way!"

Amongst their muttering, the group began to disperse, but Dandy Lee still wouldn't pull into the drive. Samson motioned her, and the town car hesitantly began to move, snapping tar bubbles under its whitewalls. Samson limped inside, slammed the door, and came face to face with Zassy and Frank in the foyer.

Samson thrust a thumb over his shoulder and glared at Zassy. "You take care of Dandy Lee!" He turned on Frank. "And you. I want you in the study. Now."

Frank nodded and disappeared down the hall.

"What's goin on?" Alice called from the top of the stairs.

"Get back up there!" Samson shouted. He followed Frank to the study and slammed the door behind him. "What in hell's goin on around here?" He literally shook with rage. Beside Frank, Samson realized himself no longer the tallest man at Bellwether.

"I don't know, sir," Frank replied. "Somethin happened to me. Somethin I can't explain."

"What?"

"I . . . ."

"What?"

"I . . . wept. Blood, sir."

"Bullshit. I don't believe it."

"Somethin happened, sir."

"Then do it."

"Excuse me, sir?"

"Do it. Cry. I wanna see for myself."

"But sir, I can't."

Samson let out a victorious laugh. "Of course you can't. So why all them niggers down there wanna see you?"

Frank didn't reply.

"Anybody comes back around, you run 'em off, understand?"

"Yes, sir."

"I'm not gonna have some–some goddamn–freak-show. I won't tolerate it."

"Yes, sir."

"It's a disgrace. It's a goddamn disgrace."

"Yes, sir."

"You ain't gonna be runnin your mouth about this, either. You got that? I hear Alice say one word–" Samson broke off and lowered his voice. "And you're a dead nigger, got it?"

It started to rain by the time Jolene returned home from the big house. The weather and the weight of her massive bosom made her back ache. Some days the ache was so bad she couldn't stand straight without pain, and at times, her circulation seemed nonexistent, the tips of her fingers often numb. Fat droplets dampened the gray in her hair, thunder rumbled through the pine flats, faint but insistent.

She closed the door against the breeze behind her, swiped the rain from her brow, and saw Frank and Zassy at the kitchen table, the oil lamp burning high between them. Neither of them spoke as Zassy nervously folded a newspaper clipping.

"What's that?" Jolene asked.

"Nothin." Zassy's gaze fell to the blue-yellow flame flickering in the lamp.

"What's it say?"

"Mama," Frank said. "She wants to send me away."

"What?"

"She said I don't belong here anymore."

"Frank!" Zassy said.

"Well, it's true, ain't it?"

"What's got into you?" Jolene said, panic turning to anger. "What are you talkin about, sendin Frank away?"

"I've been thinkin." Zassy looked up. "I been readin in the paper about a man in New Orleans. I think he can help Frank."

"What man? Where you been readin?"

Zassy unfolded the clipping and pressed it flat on the table. Jolene picked it up and read the article circled near the bottom:

MISSIONARY OF RENOWN OPENS BIBLE COLLEGE. Sherman Strong offers curriculum for ministerial candidates at 626 Dauphine.

"I wanna do this for my boy," Zassy said. "I want him to understand what God done to him. I want Frank to make somethin of himself." She lowered her head. "I want him to find some peace."

"I think you're bein selfish," Jolene said. "I think maybe you're the one who can't deal with it, and every time you look at your boy you're reminded."

Zassy didn't reply.

"Mama?" Frank reached across the table and took his mother's hand in his own. "If it's what you want, I'm willin to consider it. Write him a letter. Ask him if he takes coloreds. See what he has to say."

"But what do *you* wanna do, Frank?" Jolene asked.

"I wanna do what's right." He let go his mother's hand, and stood. "I'm gonna go pray. I'm gonna go pray for an answer." He reached for his Bible, slid it under his shirt, and stepped out into the rain.

* * *

Teense dreamt. She walked again, as in the days before the stroke, moving from room to room. Without effort she walked then, before the canes and before the wheelchair, too difficult to maneuver in and out of now. In the dream, she looked behind door after door, inspected each corner, left no closet unopened. She remembered every detail, from the faded floral wallpaper to the ugly brown water stains that spread in the ceiling after the rains of '27.

She flung the front door wide and bobbed into the sun, warm and familiar on her face. She hadn't realized how much she missed it until she felt herself penetrated by the muggy heat. Let people talk about how they couldn't stand the heat and humidity. The sticky air clung to you and made you uneasy, so you never went soft.

She looked down and saw herself as a girl with beribboned pigtails and scuffed shoes, which meant one thing: War. Never in the years before or since the War of Northern Aggression did she wear tattered shoes. And her dress: Mama stitched it together from sackcloth when the golden eagle coins ran out.

The sound of horses came from a distance. Teense peered through a patch of crepe myrtle and saw the advance of troops, men in gray, man and beast charged with the determination to fight change. She ran to meet them in a hazy field of yellow flowers, but uncertainty overcame her as the charge stormed toward her, and a death-like rhythm of hooves ate away at the ground.

The officers reined their horses and pulled up beside her.

"Teense?" came a haunted voice from above.

She peered up the length of the horse to its rider, bending toward her, blocking out the sun.

"Daddy."

She knew she wasn't a little girl anymore, knew the war was over, knew Daddy was dead. What could it mean other than his spirit had come to take her to heaven?

She reached for his polished boots and trouser legs, and he lifted her beside him.

"Why did you come for me, Daddy?" Teense grasped at the golden epaulets on his shoulders. "Where's Jesus?"

"Hush now, little Teense girl." He shushed her with a white-gloved finger to his lips, his eyes cautious in the shade under the loose brim of his Colonel's chapeau.

The horses and the silent, faceless soldiers on all sides grew restless, eager to race on to battle and dubious victory. Daddy urged his horse across the breach of pale yellow flowers, the ghostly troop in his traces, toward a stand of oak, wavering in the faded light from a starched sunset, a blanched breeze. And soon, the very sound of the march itself was swallowed up into the sun-bleached memory of time.

Dawn broke before Frank returned to an empty house. Trousers damp, he'd stripped his shirt and bundled his Bible inside it to guard against the rain. He'd made a deal with God.

Give me a sign. If it's blood, Thy will be done.

He walked through an empty house to his room, laid on the bed, and watched the sun rise over the tops of the pine and fir outside the window, a blood-red eye swirling in a soft, blue sea.

He brought his hands to his chest, cleared his mind and drew breath, opened his soul to God. His cheeks and ears burned, a gorge rose in his throat. He wanted to weep. A great love grew in the aura of the spirit that enveloped him, a love reducing his body to nothing, freeing his soul.

I am yours, my God. Thy will be done.

God came so quickly, eyes mirrors to the sorrows and joys, suffering and triumph, of the ages. All-knowing. All-consuming. All creation in a depthless whirlpool of infinite time.

My God. I am Your servant.

Frank's spirit rose from the physical world toward the Everlasting. Even so, he still felt the fountain of tears bubbling within, expansive with the hope and love from On High. A tear trembled at the corner of his right eye, rumbled with a volcanic force, ready to burst in an ardent spray of blood-lava. It seeped from the lid, scalded the tender tissue.

This is the sign. No more questions. Thy will be done.

He forced his spiritual reach into the tips of his earthly hand and relied on God to guide it to his face. The tips of his fingers prickled as if he'd skimmed a pot of boiling water.

I am Yours.

Yet when he drew back his hand, there was no blood.

And suddenly, there was no God.

His spirit plummeted, tumbled him back onto the mattress. Uncertainty snaked its way into his brain.

"Frank!" Zassy called from outside. "Frank!"

He couldn't answer. His vision had been nothing more than an hallucination. He'd conjured God out of his own weakness. It wasn't a sign. He hadn't even come close to the communion with the Lord he'd imagined. There could be no more tears from this day forward. He heard the front door thrown wide and Zassy's quick footsteps.

"Frank!"

"What is it, Mama?" The rough edges of his voice smoothed. He assuaged himself with the resolution not to shed the tears, and gathered strength from within–not God's, but his own.

"It's Miss Teense." Zassy stood in the doorway, her face ashen. "She's dead."

* * *

The murmur of the small crowd rose and fell across the distance separating Frank, Zassy and Jolene from the funeral in the Whites Only section of the cemetery. The rusted fence dividing the grounds north to south placed the coloreds to the west. But it was from the west the Lord would one day come marching. When the services were over and the white mourners left, the three would get their chance to pay last respects.

"Hmmph." Jolene was indignant, dressed in black from the pillbox hat on her head to the long skirt at her thick ankles. "Just look at that crew. There's not one of them politicians or lawyers or their women-folk who loved that woman any more than we did, and we gotta stand outside."

"They loved her," Zassy said. "Even though they didn't know her as well as we did." Concealed in mourning lace, she adjusted the black veil and pulled the dark gloves tight over her fingers.

Frank gazed over the rusted ironwork, saw men wearing black suits much like his own, women in funereal finery, gathered beside a granite tomb with the word BOUDREAUX chiseled in high Roman lettering.

Samson shook hands, his voice echoing across the cemetery. He might be in mourning, but a funeral could also be a convenient place to grandstand. Marie sat quietly in a row of folding chairs around Teense's black lacquer coffin, shaded by a blue-striped, canvas awning.

Brother Kyle of the First Baptist Church of Lake Charles took his place and the crowd's murmurs waned.

"Ask and it shall be given you," Brother Kyle said. "Seek and ye shall find. Knock and the door shall be opened unto you."

The Book of Matthew. Frank knew the words. Brother

Preston had been fervent in his devotion to the message of love in its chapters, his favorite recounting of the crucifixion and the resurrection. Then a faint breeze echoed with the ancient voices of Corinthians.

"Behold, I show you a mystery; we shall not all sleep, but we shall all be changed, in a moment, in the twinkling of an eye, at the last trump: for the trumpet shall sound and the dead shall be raised incorruptible, and we shall be changed."

Frank saw Alice bow her head, thick blonde locks spilling in a cascade of gold from beneath her veil.

" . . . . for we wrestle not against flesh and blood, but against principalities, against powers."

Frank looked up to the high, white clouds over the cemetery.

Alice.

You can protect her.

By leavin.

Alice.

You can save her.

And yourself.

Three days later, the first of the guests arrived for the charity dinner, preceded by the yaps of dogs. At the hateful sounds of barking, Samson's temper flared. He threw down his newspaper and limped to the front door.

Two automobiles pulled up in front. Claude and Ethan Lermontant, along with their Irish Setters, rode in a black motorcar, complete with high running boards and streamlines. The second automobile belonged to Dooley: a red, six-cylinder Stutz Bearcat with balloon tires. Another young man rode with him, a boy Samson didn't recognize.

"Over there!" Samson waved his arm in a broad sweep toward the open field to the east. "And tie up those damn dogs!" Claude thought the breed a superior hunter, but Samson thought they were the stupidest animals he'd ever laid eyes on.

Claude waved back, the brim of his straw hat bobbed. Sun glanced off oval frames, teeth gleamed. He motioned for Dooley to back up, and the grinding of gears meshed with the urgency of the dogs' barking.

The Bearcat rolled down the drive and lurched toward the grass. Claude's car followed suit, and both found a spot in the far corner near the remnants of the old cookhouse. The lumber long since carted off, there remained only crumbled brick and a cracked stone foundation, from which a scrubby blackberry bush sprang. The dogs came out of the automobile in a russet blur. They barked louder, dug their noses into the ground and ran in frantic circles.

"Mornin, Mister Lermontant, sir." Frank walked up to welcome the guests.

"Who's that? Who's that nigger there?" Possessed of Southern bravado, blustery and aggressive in both argument and polite conversation, Claude appeared dapper in his white linen planter's suit, but he brushed a dusting of red fur from the sleeves.

"Frank, sir, and mighty glad ya'll could come on down."

"Why that's a powerful cheerful attitude to have there, boy. What say you go rustle up them dogs and get 'em settled down? Could you do that?"

"Yes, sir."

The men made their way to the house. Ethan, Dooley, and the new boy headed for a side door, but Claude ventured toward the verandah and Samson.

"Heya, Boudreaux."

"Goddammit, Claude. I told you not to bring those–those goddamn–dogs."

Claude raised his hands, palms flat. "We couldn't leave 'em alone all day and all night. They'll be fine." He lowered his hands inside his jacket pockets. "We'll let 'em run this afternoon. Sun'll wear 'em out. I'll take care of 'em."

"You damn well better."

"Got that nigger of yours tyin 'em up right now."

"You keep those boys of yours away from him, too. I don't want no trouble."

"Boudreaux." Claude grinned. "You growin soft on niggers?"

Samson felt the forked vein throb on his forehead. "What in hell are you doin here anyway? It ain't even noon yet."

"It's that boy of mine." Claude grinned and his glasses slanted sideways across his face. "I think he's still got a shine on Miss Alice."

"Who's that other boy?"

"They're roommates down at Tulane. That there's Ronnie Mitchell from over at Lafayette. Folks are oil people. Well, petroleum refinin. Remember when I bunked with you that semester in Baton Rouge? That was some days, yeah?"

"Ones I'll never forget."

"Ronnie's on the boxin team with Dooley."

"You think I don't have enough mouths to feed without you bringin in all the stragglers?"

"Heya, Boudreaux!" Claude raised his hands again. "He's a good kid. Maybe he ain't got the good breedin we do down here, but his family's a decent lot."

"What's wrong with his nose? The rest of his kin look like that?"

"Broke it. Way I heard tell is he was sparrin with another kid one day and the other fella just off and popped him. Bam!" He snapped a fist into his palm and smiled.

"Why'd he do that? That kid provocate him?"

"Naww, he's just a little overeager, I guess."

A spasm of barking came from the rear of the house.

"See, Boudreaux?" Claude said. "Sounds like that

nigger of yours got everything under control. Now you just relax." He placed a hand at Samson's shoulder. "And maybe we can look over your case statement for the fundraiser, whatta ya say?"

Samson shrugged off Claude's hand and limped inside. There, he saw Alice on the landing. She wore a pale green sundress, and talked to the new boy with the Tulane crest on his shirt, jet hair oiled and parted from the right. Ethan and Dooley slumped against the sides of the entryway. Dooley seemed perplexed.

Samson grew leery. A lady didn't meet potential beaux in such a manner. She stood away, at a distance, her back against the wall. And she talked with her eyes. It was the lack of a good mother, Samson reasoned, and this infuriated him more.

"Alice!"

All eyes turned on him.

"What?"

"Go–find your mother."

"Why?"

"Because I said so and that's all you need to hear."

A heated silence followed before she resigned. "All right." She took a step up and turned. Her gaze met the new boy's brown eyes. "Nice to meet you."

"Nice to meet you, Miss Alice."

Life came into her step as she sprang to the top of the stairs and disappeared. The boys stared after her, betrayal ugly on Dooley's face.

"Heya, boy," Claude said. "This here's Representative Boudreaux, our fine host. You shake his hand, son. And that there's Ronald Mitchell, Samson."

Ronnie moved forward and extended his hand. "Pleasure, sir."

Samson took the boy's grip in his own and asserted pressure, but he felt the boy's intensifying, too. Ronnie relaxed.

A moment later, Samson let go. He smiled. A handshake could say more than hours of the most tedious conversation.

"That's a beaut there, boy." He pointed at Ronnie's nose. "Claude says you broke it in the boxin ring, that so?"

"Yes, sir."

"So, you're a boxer, eh?"

"Ronnie's on the boxin team with me, Samson," Dooley said.

"Is that so? And what do you learn on this boxin team of yours, Dooley? Do you learn not to address your elders in the proper manner?"

"No, sir."

"That's better." Samson turned back to Ronnie. "Claude tells me you hail from Lafayette, that true?"

"Yes, sir."

"Says your folks are oil people, that correct?"

"Yes, sir."

Samson talked as he limped away. "And how long you been boxin?"

"Uh, five years, sir," he replied.

"Go on," Claude told Ronnie with a swish of the hand.

So Ronnie followed Samson slowly as Claude's voice echoed behind them:

"Samson said he don't want no trouble out of you two, so just go on and stay out of the way. And stay away from that nigger, too, hear?"

Samson released Ronnie from the study an hour later after pumping him for information. His family had migrated from the Carolinas with the oil boom after the century mark. He was an only child who aspired to professional boxing, along with a degree in business, to ready him for the day he would take hold of his inheritance. Ronnie was polite and sharp, and Samson seemed pleased.

Ronnie walked down the long corridor giving way to the dining room on the right and the kitchen doors to the left, behind which he heard coloreds' voices. He paused at the entryway and gazed up the empty stairs before opening the front door and stepping outside.

Alone on the verandah, he overlooked several acres giving way to a private street at the bottom of a steep slope. The waves of heat from the road danced in the sun past the shade of an oak, limbs heavy with the weight of moss. To the east, he'd learned, past the field where they parked, lay Bellwether's boundary. Acres to the west it stretched, too. To the north, a bend in the Calcasieu River defined the plantation's limits. The tall pines at the reaches of the property kept omnipotent vigil.

The dogs barked. Ronnie stepped off the verandah and walked across the lawn toward the empty field from where the sounds had come. He brushed past the twisted tendrils of the blackberry bush and spied Ethan and Dooley. Several feet away, the Irish Setters were trying to scale a pine tree. And the colored boy clung to a limb near the top.

"Dooley!" he shouted.

Dooley turned on the balls of his feet. "Come on, Ron!" Laughter broke from the back of his throat.

Ronnie walked up beside Dooley, his gaze riveted to the colored boy's in the tree. The dogs' yaps rang hollow on the tepid air.

"This here's what we call 'treein the nigger'," Dooley said. "Whatta you think about that?"

"I think you're mighty stupid, Dooley. Mighty stupid."

Dooley's chin swelled, his eyes glinted with flecks of chipped diamond. "Not stupid enough to make moves on his best friend's girl!" He aimed a punch in Ronnie's direction, but Ronnie stepped back and slammed Dooley between the eyes with a curled-up fist. Blood showered from Dooley's nose.

"Oww!" he screamed. "What the fuck you do that for?"

"Cause you're a fuckin idiot, Dooley."

"Goddammit!" Samson roared from behind.

Ronnie turned, saw Samson waving his cane beside the blackberry bush. Claude appeared behind him as two black, frightened faces appeared at the kitchen glass. Engines revved at the end of the drive: delivery trucks, laden with the tent and more chairs. The escalating volume of noise rose to a deafening pitch.

And from an upstairs window, Alice screamed.

IV

Time disintegrated into barren plains of faith. Frank moved during the daylight hours, following the sun that beckoned him into the wilderness, that exiled him from a physical world he could see and hear, smell and touch. Some days the pull strong, his direction clear, others were clouded with doubt when no sign came that God acknowledged his existence.

His shirt and trousers smelled of the day's sweat, soiled from lying on the ground at night, his shoes soggy from marsh and rain, and the stitching began to give from daily strain. Bible damp from the clutch of his fingers, the pages curled, his grip visible in the indentations of the leather. He'd taken nothing with him into this world other than the clothes on his back and his Bible. He was vulnerable to a God Who took delight in tormenting him.

I have no peace, no quietness; I have no rest, but only turmoil.

Susceptible to the physical world, Frank soon felt safer traveling under cover of darkness. The daylight hours were all too often filled with taunts of hatred, spilling on the breeze from passing automobiles, sometimes with physical pain when hurled bottles or rocks found their mark. So he took to the wood and the bayou.

He found rabbits and fish to eat, learned patience in stalking them, and found peace in the wisdom granted him to fashion weapons. He learned persistence in tapping flints to create the fire. However, once he'd acquired two good rocks, their weight in his pocket, along with the press of the wooden spike strapped at his side, began to trouble him: they represented his dependence on a world he wanted to escape. So he gave them up, and his stomach grew emptier.

Fasting, he felt, would help break his hold on the physical world, would render his mortal needs useless, and in so doing, he might commune closer with God. On nights when his belly grumbled and he lay weak from lack of food, the stars swirled within reach, the heavens declared the glory of God, the skies proclaimed the work of His hands. The universe spun only for Frank:

I find You, O Lord, in everything beautiful and wicked in this world. I feel Your presence in the reflection of light over the water. I sense Your closeness in the wounded cypress, like great gnarled fists risin up to the sky in defiance. You are the sun devourin the mornin mist, warmin the blood, invadin my lungs with Your breath. So close, yet still my heart aches for You to fill it.

For it was faith, ultimately, that drove him to seek God amidst a forsaken world.

Hungrier, weaker.

Frank gave up the remnants of his shoes and the soles of his feet grew tough and callused, crackling over dead limbs, snapping the underbrush with a steady, progressive stride. He didn't yet know where God led him or why, but he felt certain his exodus from Bellwether had been preordained. He couldn't have stayed there, couldn't have hoped to overcome the humiliation he'd suffered for all to witness. Especially Alice, who'd seen him stripped of all dignity.

North of Breaux Bridge on Bayou Teche, Frank suffered a setback when a discarded ax blade caught his bare foot by surprise. Stained by the elements, the instrument's edge had remained sharp enough to slice open the skin in the arch of his right foot.

He limped to the water, plunged a hand into the thick mud at the bottom, scooped up the muck, and brought a cool poultice to the wound, the shock quick and unmerciful. He tore a strip of denim from the frayed hem of his breeches and tied it around the wound, then limped in search of a branch he might use for a crutch.

He found a sturdy oak limb and set about the meticulous task of chipping away at the bark. Soon, he'd fashioned a smooth support for his arm, but the branch's weight made it clumsy. He found a smaller branch in hopes of making a cane, but even so, it would be days before his foot could find the ground without opening the flesh.

He slept. And the voice of the prophets called to his soul from unremembered times:

Nor height, nor depth, nor any other creature, shall be able to separate us from the love of God.

When he awoke near morning, the shadows crept away, fled from dawn. The world, inky and black, gave way to the clarity of day. In this quietude before the rest of the world awakened, Frank felt the presence of God close at hand, and he begged:

Show me Thy ways, O Lord; teach me Thy paths. Lead me in Thy truth and teach me: for Thou art the God of my salvation; on Thee do I wait all the day.

As the sun pierced the thick veil of fog and broke into radiant shafts of light over the bayou, Frank prayed. The world dissolved to gray, then gave way to color. Faded hues came to life with an ever more vibrant cast: the prickly green of fir, the decayed brown of fallen leaves, bursts of vivid color from wildflowers growing along the banks of the river. The chorus of night waned as the rest of the world awakened, the water alive with the sound of splashing.

He'd never rebuild his strength, never heal, if he didn't eat. So he caught two fish, spearing them through with a slender branch, found wood for a fire, and soon had flame. He ate, peering out at the bayou. If only Bayou Teche was the great river that gave way to the Kingdom. If only he could plunge into the tide without worry and float safely and serenely on its current.

Moments later, he seized the blade, took the branch he'd intended for a cane, and struggled to fit them together. Flimsy, but it would work. And by noon, he cut half the wood he needed to make a raft. He worked into the night when he finally rested again, and gave thanks.

Two days later, he was on the water.

The current pushed him along, unhurried, toward an unknown destination. Frank grew feverish, unable to keep down anything he ate, whether from the water or from the shore. The sun flamed without mercy during the first two days, and the third night grew colder as infection set in. Oblivious to the world around him, but assured the hand of God guided him, Frank hugged the raft as it pitched lazily underneath.

And next morning, unconscious, he floated into an outcropping of dead branches and reeds, unaware of the harbor where he docked, or of the eyes there that spied him.

"Do you think he's dyin?"

Frank became aware of a girl's voice, realized the rocking motion had stopped beneath him, then became aware of the pain. It raged through his body as the nerves woke. A groan built in his gut, but he didn't know if he had the strength to push it out.

"Don't be scared." A man's voice. "He's just comin around."

Vision blurred, Frank's eyes crackled open. Another soft groan died in the back of his throat.

"You're all right now. Can you hear me? You're all right. Somebody lookin for ya?"

"No–" He coughed. "–sir." He focused on the roof of a porch, saw a small, honeycombed wasp's nest.

"Then how come you're out on the river on that thing in the shape you're in?"

A gaunt black man, arms behind his back, face seeming somehow like a mask, stood before a wall of unpainted shingle-board held together with tar.

"I'm–" But no matter what he said would sound unbelievable. A dull ache wrapped around Frank's heart, ready to spill with his burdened love of God, yet wary of what the man's reaction would be. "God–" He coughed again.

"Does it still hurt?"

"Yes–sir."

"Aisha washed out your foot while you were asleep. You was just crawlin with infection. Mighty surprised you didn't wake up when that sour mash hit your foot." His brow lowered, and welts grew on his forehead. What was it about his face? It seemed held together with tar, too. "Name's Drumson. Davis Drumson. Sorry you gotta sleep out here on the porch, but you're probably better off."

A black girl came into Frank's line of vision. Stocky and wide-hipped, her chest and face were rather flat. She offered him a meek smile, averted her gaze, and shuffled a solid leg.

"This here's Aisha," Davis said. "My daughter. She found ya."

"Thank ya," Frank murmured. "Are there others?"

"Other what?" Davis asked.

"People."

"Just me and Aisha, that's all." He lowered his gaze. No eyebrows. That's what it was about him. No eyelashes, either.

"I'm mighty grateful to you both," he replied, consciousness slipping. "I'm Frank. Frank Potter."

"You hardly touched your supper," Aisha said. She stood on the porch near Frank's feet, the sun low in the western sky at her back.

"I'm not very hungry," he replied.

"You need to eat somethin, though. You need to get your strength back."

"I've been . . . fastin, too. Sometimes, even when I wanna eat I can't."

"Fastin?"

He nodded.

"You mean, not eatin anything?"

He nodded again.

"Why you wanna do somethin like that?"

"Because."

"Well?"

"Because it's what God wants." There, he'd said it.

"God told you not to eat anything?" Aisha laughed, sparkles of light in the midst of her darkened face. "That's a good one."

"I'm bein honest with you."

"Honest? How?"

"Tellin the truth. At least, it's what I believe to be the truth."

"What makes you so special anyhow?"

"Special? I don't know." Frank crossed an arm over his chest and closed his eyes.

"What was you doin out there, anyway?"

"Lost," he murmured. "I was lost."

"But you're found now," she replied with certainty.

"No."

"What do you mean? No? I found you. I brought you up here."

"I ain't thanked you enough." He opened his eyes.

"Thanked us plenty, I reckon." She smiled. "I was just bein mean. Daddy said he figured you're runnin from the police. What'd you do?"

"I ain't committed a crime I know of."

"Must have done somethin." Aisha moved to the side, propped her short, stout frame against a wooden post and crossed her arms over her flat chest. "You were in awful desperate shape for a man ain't done nothin. You can tell me. I won't say nothin to Daddy. I promise."

"Little girl, if you're hopin to hear me say I killed a man or broke out of jail, you're gonna be mighty disappointed."

"Uh-huh. So you killed somebody and broke out of jail."

Frank chuckled, revived.

"What's so funny? You laughin at me?"

"I ain't laughin at you. I just think it's funny, that's all."

"What?"

"Your romantic notions."

"If you weren't so sick I'd kick ya, I swear!"

Frank laughed. "You thought I meant 'romantic' a different way."

"Now you callin me dumb? I know what romantic is. You think I'm sweet on ya. Well I ain't!"

The river rushed low under the cricket-song. From far away came the hollow call of a crane. Aisha shuffled to the opposite end of the porch and faced the bayou.

"All those things you was sayin about God tellin ya not

to eat," she said, "it really true?"

"Yes."

"I believed in God once, before He done what He did to Daddy and took Mama away."

"Your mama, she passed?"

"Naww, she ain't dead, just run away."

"What happened to your daddy?"

Aisha turned. "Ain't you noticed?"

"What?"

"His face. His hands."

"No."

"You ain't seen his hands? You ain't noticed his–?"

"No."

"Well . . . ."

"What is it?"

"Better let him tell ya. He'll be comin in soon. Always disappears come evenin. Don't know where he goes, what he does, just know he goes . . . ." Her voice trailed into a whisper, then she spoke up again. "Hey, you gonna eat your supper or not? Ain't eatin it because you know, do ya?"

"Know?"

"About us."

"Don't follow ya."

"Never mind."

"I'm grateful for the food, I really am, it's just my appetite ain't up yet."

"You ain't just makin that up?"

"Of course not. Why would I lie to you? You saved me."

Aisha smiled, but it faded, lost to the lengthening shadows. "You weren't makin up the other, either, about God and all?"

Frank grew quiet.

"You really think God talks to you?"

Silence.

"I never heard Him," she went on. "I done a lot of prayin for Daddy, but He ain't never talked out loud to me."

"It ain't like talkin out loud," Frank replied, his body inundated with a sudden assuring numbness. "I've asked Him to speak to me out loud, but He never does. He speaks to me in here." He tapped his chest with a finger. "Where's my Bible? It get . . . lost?"

"No chance of that. You was holdin on so tight, I thought I'd never wrestle it outta your hands."

"Where is it?"

"Above your head."

Frank craned his neck and saw the Bible several inches from him. With relief, he reached for its marred leather.

"You ain't gonna start readin to me are ya? You ain't a preacher or somethin, are ya?"

"No, I ain't gonna read it now. I just wanna know it's near."

"You hold a mighty big stock in a book."

"Ever read it?"

"No. I know a lot about it, though. Mama made us go to church when I was little. I know all about God and Jesus."

"What do you know?"

"Thought you said you ain't gonna start preachin." Suspicion rose in her voice and her posture grew guarded.

"I ain't."

"Well, I'm goin back in anyway. Want me to leave your supper, in case you change your mind?"

"That's all right, you can take it with ya."

She shuffled to Frank's side, bent to pick up the tin plate full of cornpone in molasses and cold chicken, then disappeared inside.

Some time after dark, Frank heard the boards groan, opened his eyes, and spied a large blackened shape hovering near the doorway.

"Aisha?"

"It's me," came Davis' voice. "Didn't mean to wake ya, I'm just goin in the house."

"Sir?"

"Yeah?" Davis turned in the shadows.

"I–wanted to tell you again how grateful I am."

"Shit, done thanked us enough, boy, now get some rest."

"Sir?"

"What is it?"

"Your daughter, she seems upset. I hope I ain't done it."

"Upset?"

"Concerned."

"About what?"

"She's got a good heart, I can tell. She's concerned for you. Are you ill, sir?"

The shadow remained unmoving in the cracks of light from inside.

"Tell me if I'm out of line," Frank said, "but I'm concerned for you, too. You're good people. You've given me comfort."

"Who are you, anyway?" Davis shuffled his feet.

"Just a man tryin to do what's right, tryin to live for God, and willin to act on how He instructs."

"Preacher, huh? I remember this happened to another colored fella in New Iberia now. White folks run him out on the rail. Beat the livin shit out of him at a prayer meetin one night, in front of all them folks, and dumped him on the Southern Pacific. Guess they would have felt a might odd doin him in, bein a preacher and all."

"I ain't a preacher, sir."

"Then who are ya?"

"Just a man," he whispered.

"Huh?"

"I believe the Lord sent me here."

"What makes you think that?"

"I've been–travelin–for a great while, tryin to find the answer to what God expects of me."

"Why?"

"The Lord has touched me."

"How?"

Frank hesitated. "Some time ago I experienced . . . the Stigmata."

"The what?"

"I–wept blood, sir. And ever since– I came into the bayou to–find Him–to–find an answer. And He sent me here."

"Blood."

"Believe me when I tell you I feel I have a purpose here. And your daughter's concern leads me to believe it's you I've been sent to learn from."

"I ain't never heard such– Blood?" The darkness made it impossible to discern Davis' features. "You're just all crazy from the fever, boy."

"Please, sir, I'm tellin you the truth. You can believe me."

"So you go off and lose yourself in the bayou? That don't sound like God tellin you to do somethin. It's foolish."

"Nothin's easy, sir. It's meant to be that way."

"Why can't it be?"

"Because what's won too easy is never appreciated. Jesus said, 'Because straight is the gate and narrow is the way, which leadeth unto life, and few there be that find it'."

"But–" Drumson's shadow moved closer. "Then you tell me why God afflicted me. Why'd He do that? I've been tryin to figure out how a God of kindness and mercy can do what He does. Takin away a man's hands, takin away his ability to make for himself, takin away his wife, takin away his daughter's happiness because she's gotta look out for him because nobody else will. You tell me what God that is, boy, I ain't figured it out yet."

Frank didn't reply.

"Dammit, boy!" Davis' words quavered under the abrasiveness. "I don't know who you are or what you're talkin about. Why you wanna start all this bull? We saved ya from the river and most likely a certain end. You can't–"

"I'm sorry if I upset you, sir."

"Stop callin me Sir. Name's Davis. I don't wanna think about things like God no more. He left me to fend for myself." He leaned against the door and the light from the kerosene lantern inside spilled into the night.

Frank blinked against the intrusion as his pupils pained into focus.

"This is what your kind, givin God did to me." Davis thrust his arms in front of him. Where his hands should be, there appeared only nubs, charred it seemed, fissured and cracked as if roasted.

"How?" Frank asked.

"Leprosy, boy, just like out of that Bible you're so fond of quotin." A mosquito buzzed near Davis' face and he raised a blackened stump to swipe it away, then thrust his arms behind his back again as if in deep thought or embarrassment. "I don't know how it happened, it just happened. Don't know who it was touched me had it, probably one of them fellas I used to work with on the oil rig out in the Gulf."

"I'm sorry."

"Sure you're sorry, everybody's sorry. Everybody's so sorry they run us out, burned the house down around us in the middle of the night. That's when Jessie said she can't take it no more. That's when she run off to her folks in Greenwood, afraid even to take her only child with her, let alone give her a kiss goodbye. What kind of God does that to a man who's honest and upright and decent, and never did smoke or drink or swear, leastways 'til this happen?"

"Aisha, she–?"

"She ain't got no sign." Davis turned away, brought his arms to the front as if to hide them, as if Frank might find the sight of them repulsive. "But we can't take no chance, ya know?"

"Daddy?" Aisha appeared in the glow of the doorway. "What's all the hollerin about? He bein mean to you, too?"

"What are you talkin about?"

"He talkin God and Jesus at ya?"

"Go on inside, girl, we're talkin private."

"He don't appreciate nothin," Aisha said. "Don't eat nothin I make him. Should have left him to the river."

"You hear me, girl. I said go on now."

Aisha lowered her gaze on Frank and a curious nervousness quivered across her cheeks before she closed the door behind her, left the world outside as vast and dark as it had been before.

"She likes you," Davis murmured. "She needs a boy to pay attention to her, she needs somebody besides me, but who's gonna? Would you, knowin what you do?"

"She's . . . got a good soul."

"You're dodgin the question. Answer truthful. This God you're tryin to find, didn't He say somethin about speakin the truth? I am the truth, somethin, somethin?"

"I am the way," Frank replied. "'I am the way, the truth and the life'."

"Then truth it is, boy, tell me straight."

The helpless, human side of Frank's brain cried that he couldn't–could not touch either of them–without fear of the risk involved. Yet another voice assured him he'd be safe from the invisible bacilli no doubt swarming their flesh.

"I . . . ain't afraid. Are you treatin it?"

Drumson turned away again, bringing his arms to the front. He moved to the end of the porch, his tread heavy on the complaining boards.

"Used to use the chaulmoogra oil for my hands, before they– After, didn't see no reason to keep it up, didn't save 'em."

"What'd it do for you, ease the pain?"

"A might. Some days I don't feel much of nothin, though, unless when I talk or eat too much. Those blamed things around my mouth. But some days it's so bad nothin's gonna do it any good. At least it ain't took my eyes yet."

"There must be somethin you can do, for the pain."

"Medicine's expensive, boy. Too expensive for a man ain't got nothin."

"You have your daughter."

"But what's she got? Nothin. No hope. No happiness. No life no more."

"Jesus said, 'Come unto me, all ye that labor and are heavy laden, and I will give you rest'."

"That's all fine and good, boy," Davis said. "But what about livin day to day, so lonesome for another human bein your heart breaks? What kind of life's that? And you, has God give you rest?" A hint of sorrow lay under the bitterness of his breath.

"Yes," Frank replied. "He has. He gave me you."

An odd quiet descended on Bellwether in the months following Frank's disappearance. Once there'd been meaning in even the most insignificant of chores, but now there was an absence of thought or care. No need to rush through dinner or hurry cleaning the big house. Useless looking forward to finishing up each day and returning home. In Frank's absence, the walls of the old quarter house became bleak and confining.

Zassy grew listless, quiet. The strain of worry and guilt showed in her face, her eyes: despondent and dull, the eyes of an old woman. When Jolene caught the lackluster glaze in Zassy's once vibrant black eyes, she wanted to tell her that she'd brought it all upon herself. But Jolene didn't. Couldn't.

Alice graduated near the top of her class in May, wrote Ronnie once a week and called him twice on weekends. When Samson caught her pouring over an application to Tulane, he said he wouldn't pay her tuition, that she didn't need to continue her education, since a woman's place is, of course, in the home.

So Alice found a job ringing up groceries at the A&P downtown. Samson grew furious when his secretary told him what a beautiful and pleasant daughter he'd raised, so good with the customers. It embarrassed him that she worked like common folk when she had all she'd ever require at home. Alice told him she'd quit only if he allowed her to pursue school. She said she had every intention of attending, even if it meant having to collect every cent for herself.

When Alice asked Jolene about Frank, she was told he'd gone to seek the Lord. Jolene also talked about Sherman Strong and the rectory north of New Orleans, but never actually used Frank or Sherman in the same sentence.

And certainly glad Frank was gone, although someone else had to be hired for the upkeep, Samson ignored the worry on Zassy and Jolene's faces. But on occasion, he awoke from a troubled sleep:

Blood. Christ's blood. Raining from Frank's eyes. Falling into a bloody river. Flooding the bayou and plain. Drowning every man, woman and child in its path.

But of one thing, Samson was certain:

God is not *a nigger.*

Three months passed since Frank came to the Drumson's shack on the edge of the river. His recuperation lent itself to long periods of time alone, communing with God, making peace with the world around him. He fasted occasionally, though not of his own volition.

Davis grew alarmed at Frank's condition. Although the boy seemed to have high spirits, he was sluggish with the chores: chopping firewood, gathering crawfish nets. His eyes were vacuous, his hair longer; rather than curling tight against itself, the waves relaxed and reached toward his shoulders. And the new beard did little to conceal his hollow cheeks, his transparent lips. Body skeletal, his ribs shuddered beneath the brown skin of his chest, yet the muscles along his arms remained lean and sinewy.

The company pleased Davis, even if Frank had some sort of religious complex. Perhaps he thought that by saving others, he could save himself. At first, Davis balked at the ideals and philosophies falling from Frank's tongue with such alacrity, but in time, he began to take consolation in them. Once the days seemed to be an eternity of interminable suffering, but now he'd discovered joy in rising early, walking outside, and taking in the dawn of each new day granted him, curious about the glories of the world:

"Thank You, God," he murmured as a morning ritual, "for givin me another day."

Some mornings, Davis found Frank asleep on the porch, other mornings he found the pallet deserted. But no matter where Davis chose to take his walk–along the edge of the river or through the dense wood giving way to marsh further south–he was never able to find him. Regardless, Frank always showed up before nine o'clock, ready to begin the day's work he considered his duty.

"Done missed your breakfast again!" Aisha shouted at him on more than one occasion. "And I ain't fixin you another one!" Possessed early of the realities of life, she only seemed to show hatefulness as a means to define her existence.

But Frank only smiled, a dream-induced grin, as if just awakened from heavy sleep.

Aisha cursed his indifference. Didn't he realize his presence alone was torture? She wished he'd leave, take back to the river where he came from and float away.

Henhouse cleaned, roof patched, brush cleared, the fruits of labor from the extra pair of hands raised Davis' spirits. And the pustules that stained the corners of his mouth started to fade, along with the pain in his arms and legs.

However, it wasn't all work on Bayou Teche. Chores did come to completion, even if only for a few hours. Porch swept, supper dishes washed, everything in its place, the day's burdens lifted, the body and soul in transition.

Davis and Frank sat and talked on the porch. Sometimes, Aisha wandered out to watch the sun drowning in a fiery sea, to listen to Frank's Bible stories with feigned attention–while she yearned to touch him. But if she did, she knew she'd explode into a hundred tiny pieces.

"There's a fella I used to work with out in the Gulf on that oil rig," Davis said. "He told me a story about another feller used to live in the woods of Mississippi, and every night, he'd come sneakin into town and breakin into the house where this little girl was sleepin. He said every night that man did things to that little girl and told her he was Jesus. Told her to touch the wound in his side where the Romans run him through. And after he done that to the poor child and said 'Jesus says don't tell', he'd make himself at home and get a bite to eat. There was several folks seen him leave by the front door come mornin. Said they didn't think nothin about it, though. Said they thought the child's mama had a new beau. Caught up to him eventually, though, strung out on junk he was, screamin the needle was his god . . . ."

And that night, Aisha dreamt about a man standing in the darkened corner of her bedroom. Dressed in flowing white robes, he crept from the shadows and into the moonlight draped across the end of her bed. Overjoyed and frightened at once, she knew who he was and why he'd come. He raised his hands into the silver light from outside and there, too, in his palms, glimmered moonbeams filtered through ragged holes in his flesh. His garment fell from his shoulders; he stood naked, bathed in the soft glow.

Aisha raised her gaze to his face, discerned a scruffy beard in the shadows, and eyes that imprisoned her with a love from beyond the reaches of the earth. She choked on a warm flood churning into her throat as he pulled her against him, her cheeks simmering against the cool flesh at his belly.

"I love you, Aisha," he murmured.

"Frank," she whispered.

Six months passed. As the temperature fell off, Frank began to gain weight again: his cheeks filled out under a thickened beard, eyes less distant. As Christmas approached, his thoughts turned to Bellwether. He wrote a letter to his mother, but learned the nearest post office was in Jeanerette.

Davis offered to let Frank drive his old Packard–rusted from neglect, coated with dust and pollen–if he could get it running, that is. The automobile coughed, balked and sputtered, refused to turn over. Until finally, a foul black cloud sprayed from the exhaust.

Sheriff Sonny Pollitt felt drowsy. Breakfast and lunch at the Bar-None Diner sat like a stone in his big belly, strained the material over his uniform shirt. He'd loosened his belt after a third helping of boudin, but the spicy sausage still played hell with his ulcers.

He pulled his black and white cruiser onto a wide gravel drive, waited for the old gray Packard to pass before he pulled back out onto the road, and glanced at his watch. Wire-framed glasses slid down his nose. He pushed the frames up with a thick finger. And couldn't believe what he saw. Was that old man Drumson sitting in the back seat?

He pulled out behind the automobile, but kept his distance, following it into town: past the hardware and the five and dime, the shoe shop and the bank, until finally, the Packard stopped in front of the post office.

Pollitt parked several feet away and saw a tall, grizzled, colored man emerge from the driver's seat. He looked like a wild man with that scraggly beard and all that hair.

Should have run 'em out sooner. Should have shunted 'em to Carville a long time ago.

Now there was probably a whole colony of nigger-lepers living out by the river. Pollitt's stomach winced.

Dusk fell by the time they returned home. Comely in her best dark blue dress, Aisha was first out the door, the glow of her smile drawing attention from her flat profile. She'd talked about preparing a special dinner on the drive home, to celebrate actually seeing a little of the world again, and she seemed eager to start on the jambalaya.

"Want to sit a spell, boy?" Davis asked. "Most likely be some time before supper's ready."

"No, sir," Frank replied. "I'd like to be by myself for a while if you don't mind."

"Nah, go on," Davis said. "Just be back by supper. You know how she gets." He winked.

"I'll be back." Frank smiled.

He made his way to a clearing a quarter mile deep into the copse he regarded as his own, that he revered as sacred. The light grew dimmer, the sun waned orange amidst the trees. A circle of tall pines surrounded the cloister, blanketed with fallen needles like a spongy carpet. Near one end of the clearing lay a toppled pine: his altar.

Frank rested his elbows on the bark, closed his eyes, and prayed while the natural spires of his cathedral rustled overhead. The sounds of the river, the soft rush and flow from a distance, wound its way into the sanctuary to heighten the lucidity of his mind, to help him become one with the earth and with God.

A rustle came from the limbs overhead. Then a creak and a groan of wood, as if pushed by an eerie breeze. Only there was no breeze. A cold sweat broke on his forehead. His stomach began to churn as if other souls were drowning inside him. Was this proof of God? The same awesome force that created the earth and the heavens made real? Frank opened his eyes.

And shrieked.

He crumpled back onto the cushion of pine needles from the force of a vision, crisp and real as the flickering images of the picture show, so horrifying surely God must have turned away from it, too:

Naked and brown, Frank's feet were cracked open with an iron spike, his hands being crushed by two more spikes, a steely clang in his ear from metal against metal. His eyes burned with blood flowing from the crown of his head.

"My God," he whispered. "I–can't."

He stumbled away into the night, equilibrium nonexistent. Tall pines became living obstacles thrusting against him: a menacing maze, daring him to find his way out. The moon, frozen in a sky devoid of stars, gave no light. Faith and hope had never existed in the vast reaches of this bleak and empty plane.

Black water chokes me. Black fire burns me. Black night blinds me.

Why should I obey You? I've already given You everything. I have nothin left to take.

But my life.

Take the tremblin earth from under my feet. Take the last

remainin song in my heart. It screams like a thousand tortured birds takin flight.

Crush my joy.
Once, You were my greatest of joys.
Now, You're my greatest defeat . . . .

Dawn broke by the time Frank stumbled back to the Drumson's, an empty vessel of thought or emotion, vision hazy as if a great, shimmering-white veil lay draped over the world. He walked onto the porch, saw the door ajar. And walked inside for the first time.

A small table lay overturned, shrimp withering in umber puddles on the floor. An empty rocking chair sat under a window overlooking the river. Behind a door, he saw a single bed, unmade, and a chest of drawers with holes carved where the handles should be. Then he sensed another heartbeat besides his own, and stepped inside. He gripped the knob on a small closet door, unable to feel the sensation in his fingers. And opened it.

Pressed in the shadows, a human bulk startled and cried out, flew at him in the dim morning light.

"You!" Aisha screeched, eyes wet with fear, glimmering with rage. "Where were you? Why didn't you come? You ain't a man. You're a coward. You ain't no man of God. How could you let 'em take him? How could you?"

The river loomed in the distance, the mighty waters of the Mississippi rushing toward night and the Gulf. Carville lay just across the bridge. Frank and Aisha traveled in silence for some time, oblivious to the tattered Christmas decorations hung from electric poles in Loreauville, and depictions of the Nativity in shop windows at Laurel Ridge. She'd taken the money in Davis' savings jar, stuffed it in her skirt pocket, and insisted Frank drive.

"How do I know where Carville's at?" she'd said. "It's near Baton Rouge, so just go north. Can't you read signs?" When Frank questioned her certainty of Davis' whereabouts, she'd said, "I know. I heard Pollitt." Three men, Frank learned–a sheriff and two others–had broken in and abducted her father.

Miles of road and water fell away as Frank followed the hand that beckoned him, the hand that condemned him. Trapped inside a man he'd never wanted to be.

A group of colored men hovered by a street lamp near the corrugated corner of a small industrial plant. Soot smeared the evening sky, bled into distant darkness.

"Pull over." Aisha rolled down the window.

Frank stepped on the clutch. A disquieting mesh of metal vibrated under his foot until the automobile came to a shaky stop.

"We're lookin for the hospital," Aisha called.

A tall colored man approached, hands thrust in the pockets of faded coveralls.

"Depends," he said. "Got two. You be lookin to get doctored, south side's your bet."

"We're lookin for the one that . . . ."

The man bent at the waist and peered inside past Aisha, to Frank. "That way." He pointed down the street, straightened, and turned away.

PUBLIC HEALTH SERVICE HOSPITAL

a large sign at the entrance read.

NATIONAL LEPROSARIUM.

The car sputtered to a halt in a small parking area, deserted but for a handful of other automobiles clustered at one end of the lot. The motor died with a thump.

Hands clenched in her lap, Aisha peered at the building with fear and uncertainty: a living entity, it seemed, merely regarding them. She closed her eyes. Frank's hand, stiff and rough as sandpaper on one side, smooth as satin on the other, closed over hers. Strange waves lapped against her legs, rose toward her thick midsection, and a mythical emotion became real in her heart. Sudden strength invaded her senses. She drew breath.

"Let's go get my daddy," she said.

Medicinal and sharp, thick on the tongue, the odor of the hospital was pungent as overripe fruit. A young, red-haired nurse in starched white looked up from behind a small metal desk, a soft, river-washed glaze to her eyes. When her gaze fell on Frank, a stream wavered across the riverbed of her stare. Her heart ceased for a single beat then tripped in double-time.

"Can I help you?"

"I want my daddy," Aisha said. "I wanna see him now."

But the nurse didn't look away from Frank's disheveled appearance: rumpled clothing, strands of hair clotting at his shoulders, beard coarse and unkempt, eyes unsettling black.

"I'm sorry," she said. "No visiting hours–tonight."

"But we're takin him home," Aisha said, inconsequential in Frank's presence: a voice from some passerby echoing outside a small, contained world, spinning with the charged particles of an unseen force. A foreign love, at once inviting and dubious.

"Do you–have a release?"

"No, Ma'am. Don't need one. He ain't supposed to be

here."

"I'm–sorry–I'm–" She was retreating on the river inside her.

"Then get me someone who *does* know, ma'am."

The nurse struggled to row herself back to the shores from where her gaze fell. She lifted a shaky receiver to her ear. "Doctor Sawyer. Is he–? It's me. It's Judith. Tell him–please tell him–"

"Judy?" Another young nurse appeared, lips pursed in concern. "What is it, Hon?"

But Judith didn't reply. She dropped the receiver into its cradle.

The concerned nurse turned to Frank and Aisha. "I'm Jenny Spencer," she said with a forced smile, sincere from years of repetition. "Is there somethin I can help you with?"

"We've come to get my daddy," Aisha said. "We're takin him home."

A tall man entered the room, lean and ruddy-faced, the faint gleam of eagerness behind tired brown eyes. "What is it?" he asked.

"They say they've come to get somebody," Jenny said.

He turned to Aisha and Frank. "I'm Doctor Sawyer. Who are you here to see, Miss?"

"My daddy! How many more times I gotta say it? I just want my daddy!"

"Certainly," he replied, unaffected by her outburst. "And who might your daddy be?"

"Davis Drumson." Aisha offered a relieved smile. "He's just brung here."

"We'll see what we can find." Sawyer motioned for her and Frank to follow, and they retreated down a long, darkened corridor.

Judith propped herself against the corner of green metal file cabinet.

"Honey, you all right?" Jenny asked. "The look on

your face–"

"I thought he was . . . ."

"What?"

"I thought he was . . . ." But she couldn't finish.

The room stank of disinfectant and rot. Six beds lined the far wall under a large glass window filled with night. The fixtures overhead gave off filtered light. Three people occupied the room. Two gaunt white men wearing blue cotton robes, sat intent over a game of dominos. One looked up. Withered and slack, a large black pustule branded his cheek. His gaze moved over the doctor, the man and the girl framed in the door, then back to the game at hand. The other man, plumper, with no visible signs of infection, seemed oblivious to the visitors, the smooth ridges of his brow set in contemplation over the cross in play. And, arms thrust forward, Davis stood by the window, staring out into the night.

"Sam, Zeke. You gentlemen well this evenin?" Sawyer moved into the room.

"Fine, Doc," the fleshy man replied, eyes studious on the tiles. "Except for this cheatin bastard. Says he can keep numbers added up in his head like he's a genius or somethin. Only thing is, they're always in his favor."

Sawyer laughed.

Davis turned. His face melted like hot rubber.

Aisha rushed toward him and threw her arms around him. "It's all right, Daddy." She was trying her best not to cry, but only half succeeding. "You're comin home with us."

"Now hold on, young lady," Sawyer said. "Mister Drumson can't go home with you now, we have to run some tests first."

"You can't hold him against his will." Aisha turned red-rimmed eyes on the doctor.

"He needs to stay," Sawyer replied. "It's for his own

good."

"He's brung here against his will. You can't just lock him up."

"The man who brought your daddy here did him and you a big favor."

"He–?"

"It's not uncommon for patients to come to us this way. It–"

"So this is where you dump people nobody wants anymore," Aisha interjected.

"Honey," Davis said.

"What?" She turned on her father.

"I ain't gonna be here forever. And they're good to me. Gonna give me my own room in a day or two and–"

"You can't say you wanna stay."

"They're gonna . . . help me," he murmured.

"He needs to be here," Sawyer told her. "I assure you he's well taken care of."

Aisha folded her arms across her flat chest. "I don't believe it."

"They're gonna help me," Davis murmured again.

"We've already got him on cortisone and streptomycin treatments," Sawyer added. "He's had good reaction to the drugs, especially the sulfones."

"That don't mean nothin to me," Aisha said. She turned to an empty doorway. "Where's Frank?"

"He left," came a voice from the game-table.

Frank's shadow filled the light cast from the hallway into the room.

"Doctor?" a woman called from the darkness within, a voice ragged with pain.

Frank didn't reply.

"Doctor?" she rasped again.

* * *

Still uneasy, Judith took a tranquilizer to calm her nerves. She found her purse and walked down the empty hallway toward the exit and the parking lot, her footfalls on the tile soothing from the effects of the drug. Jenny said she'd fill in for her the rest of the night.

But she spotted a light under the door to room 3: Maddy Hearns, who should be resting after her treatment. She tapped lightly on the door.

"Miss Hearns?" she called.

"But we're likely to get funded for extensive sulfone testin soon," Sawyer said.

"You're talkin things I don't understand," Aisha replied. "And I think you're doin it to intimidate me. But I ain't gonna let ya." She peered into the hallway, looked right and left, raised her voice. "Frank!" She stepped into the deserted corridor.

"And one day when I was sixteen, about a week before the cotillion, I just bought my pretty new dress and Daddy said we were goin for a ride." A waxy sheen stained Maddy Hearns' rheumy eyes, glazed her sunken cheeks.

Frank stood over her bed.

Judith stood frozen. Staring. At him.

"It's all right." Maddy turned her head to Judith with a blissful yet unsettling smile. "Daddy said it's all right."

"You–" Judith choked. "You–aren't supposed–to be here."

Then he moved toward her. And touched her.

And a sob died in the back of Judith's throat.

* * *

When Aisha found him, five more people had gathered in Maddy Hearns' room: diseased and stricken, shadows and ghosts of former living things. Frank stood among them, silent and tall, lowering his hands to their shoulders as they cried out in pain and joy.

Aisha met his gaze, swimming in a vapid pool of wonderment, as she inhaled the odors of the room: must and decay, the sweet tang of disinfectant. Over it all, rose the smell of electricity: metallic and hot, alive on the air, charged with the steely delight of miracle.

"It *is* you," she whispered. "Ain't it?"

V

'And Jesus answering said unto them, They that are whole need not a physician; but they that are sick. I come not to call the righteous, but sinners to repentance'.

I am a man. I am an instrument.

'My flesh and my heart faileth: but God is the strength of my heart. If any man be in Christ, he is a new creature: old things are passed away, behold, all things are become new'.

At what point does the grotesque become merely grim, and when does the profane become simply ugly? For Frank, it came in moments of dark power and unyielding beauty, a suspension of time when the hour hung thick about his shoulders, lucid and tangible, like a warm rainy day or the touch of another human being. It came when he accepted the horror in his vision, and lived only to fulfill the faith of others, to follow the path already chosen for him.

'And after all that is come upon us seeing that Thou our God hast punished us less than our iniquities deserve, He hast given us such deliverance as this'.

I am chosen by God.

'Therefore, go and make disciples of all nations,

baptizing them in the name of the Father and of the Son and of the Holy Spirit, and teaching them to obey everything I have commanded you'.

I am a man.
Whom God directs.

Dear Mama and Aunt Joe,

I hope this letter finds you well. I've left the Drumson's to pursue a challenge that the Lord has set before me. He's instructed me to deliver His message, to seek out those who've strayed from Him or who've never known Him. He's shown me what must be.

Mr. Drumson was taken by force to a hospital in Carville. His daughter and I drove up to try and get him released. But something happened there. Jesus grew to live so great within my spirit that it was as if He pushed it right out of my body. I floated over myself, looked down on my body. Only it wasn't mine. It was His. And I could only watch as He blessed the sick.

Does Jesus reside in my body? Doesn't every Christian profess Jesus lives in their hearts, in their minds and souls? Yes. He is as much in them as He is in me. But for the first time, I'm aware of how close He really is. I know now for certain that He is with me always. Not a single hour goes by when I don't feel Him, become aware of Him standing at my shoulder: observing, guiding, teaching. I realize now that I needed to find out He was real. I needed proof of His existence. I believe He gave me that proof in Alexandria, but it only left me wanting more. Now that I've realized it's faith that brings Him to us, though, that He asks only for us to believe, I know He'll be with me forever.

Two months ago, the Drumson's came home when Davis' condition improved. That's when I took to the bayou, heeding His instructions, to tell what's in my heart, and people started coming from up and down the shore to hear.

During one of the services, I met a man named Simon Duchane. He told me I should be preaching regular at a spot on the bayou, and he'd help spread word of the meetings. Since then, I've held services every Sunday on the water, and every Sunday we've had a baptizing. The people who come all the time call me Bayou Jesus.

Simon has made arrangements for me to speak to his congregation on Easter. I'm sending a flyer. I'd like for you and Aunt Joe to come if Mr. Boudreaux will let you. I hope the family is doing well. I still think of Alice. I think of you, too. Maybe if things don't work out and you don't get to come for Easter, I can visit later. I love you, Mama. Aunt Joe, too.

Franklin Christian Potter

BAYOU

JESUS

4-30-37

BREAUX BRIDGE, LOUISIANA

BAYOU TECHE

CHRIST'S

HOPE

CHURCH

BAYOU

JESUS

* * *

Aisha cut Frank's hair and shaved his beard before he went away with Simon, promising her and Davis that someday he'd return. Then he bent low and brushed his lips against her cheek. A boy had come to her, a man with the stamp of greatness was leaving.

When Frank said his good-byes, picked up the suitcase the Drumson's gave him, and drove off with Simon, Aisha stared after him. And for years afterward, she stood in the same spot, waiting, knowing one day he would return. Even long after he passed into legend.

Muscles tense, Ronnie bounced on the balls of his feet, the blue silk of his shorts whispering against his legs. He threw a right cross. Harper parried. Ronnie struck another right cross. Deflected. He aimed a left hook to the jaw, but Harper ducked and his leather helmet absorbed the shock. He stumbled forward. Ronnie delivered a stiff upper cut. Harper fell to the canvas.

"That's enough," Coach Flagler said, a beefy man in a tight gray sweatshirt. "Gotta work on your defense, Harper. Good bout, Mitchell. You're puttin that cross of yours to good advantage."

"Thanks, Coach. Ronnie loosed the gloves and tugged at the helmet strap. He shook his head and speckled the canvas with sweat.

"See ya tomorrow, kids." Flagler waved and walked to his office.

Ronnie and Harper slipped through the ropes and landed on the mat, made their way to the showers in silence.

"Ronnie!"

Alice made her away across the polished gymnasium

floor. She wore a green pullover and a long black skirt.

Ronnie stopped, but Harper continued on.

"Hi, sweetheart," he said when she came beside him. Ronnie kissed her cheek, smelled the soft, clean whiff of powder mingled with tea-rose perfume. "If I didn't think you'd mind me bein all sweaty . . . ."

"You'd what?" Alice smiled.

"You know."

She sighed. "Shirley was right. Men do think about sex every seven seconds."

"You're not gonna make me wait 'til next year, are you?"

"You only pinned me at Christmas," she replied, yet the cool blue of her irises swam with promise.

Ronnie closed his eyes. His skin turned to goose flesh as the sheen of sweat cooled and prickled.

"Just be ready to go by two o'clock today." Her voice grew soft, near breathless, as she brought a finger up to the shallow cleft in his chin.

He opened his eyes. "Changed your mind about goin to Biloxi?"

"No. Daddy wants us to spend the break with him. I don't know when he ever became such a family man."

"Guess he's thinkin about makin up for lost time."

"You like Daddy, don't you?"

"Sure." Ronnie shrugged.

"He likes you, too," she said.

The wind whipped at the brim of Zassy's black straw hat as she walked past residential homes on the outskirts of Lake Charles: sidewalks cracked and broken, children playing on scrubby lawns. Blistered wood and crumbled stone gave way to the solid brick and stucco of the business district. She ducked into a damp alleyway alongside the farm supply store, the narrow corridor's cracked brick sweaty and smooth, her shortcut to the open market.

She turned left at a cross-section, stepped around several mud puddles, and came upon a row of rust-streaked trash containers, the air heavy with rot. That's when she saw the mud-speckled paper on the ground, its words a pulpy haze:

BAYOU JESUS.

She clenched her hands into fists, nails digging into the soft flesh of her palms. If this flyer had made its way into Lake Charles, how many more were there? Dread surged through her body: *A colored man people listened to. A colored man people followed.*

Her gaze traveled the alley wall, across moss growing in cracked skeins of brick, until she saw three words written in a splash of blood-red paint:

CHRIST IS COMING

"Well, if it ain't Miss Alice." Jolene wiped her hands on her apron, hugged Alice tight, then held her at arm's length. "Did you cut your hair?" she asked. "Since Christmas?"

"I just had it trimmed up." Alice slipped off her beige overcoat. "You like it?" She wore a black turtleneck sweater that brought out the blonde tumble of hair at her shoulders.

"Looks so pretty," Jolene said.

"Where's Mister Boudreaux?" Tall and road-weary, Ronnie stood over Alice's shoulder.

"In the parlor," Jolene replied. "But he said to come on down when you get here."

"You go on," Alice told him. "I want to talk to Jolene first and check on Mama."

Without a reply, Ronnie left the kitchen, and Alice turned to Jolene.

"Have you heard from Frank?" she asked.

Jolene smiled. "Oh, honey, you'd never believe it."

"What?"

Jolene glanced quickly from door to kitchen door, then produced an envelope from her apron pocket. "Don't tell Zassy I showed you this, though. She won't–"

Alice reached for the letter, read it while Jolene continued to watch the doors.

Finally, Alice looked up, her eyes curiously wide. "What happened in Alexandria?"

"The blood," Jolene murmured.

"Blood?"

A great fist squeezed Jolene's heart. Alice hadn't known. Her breath came faster along with a swift pain.

"Are you all right?" Alice stepped closer.

"I'm fine," Jolene said. "Just let me–catch my breath."

"Are you sure?"

Jolene nodded, smiled, forcing herself to take long, deep breaths until the pain diminished.

"Is this about what happened when Daddy–?" Alice's eyes grew yet wider. "It *is*, isn't it? What happened, Jolene?"

"I–shouldn't have showed it to ya, I guess. I was just so excited about everything, I–"

"You can tell me. It doesn't matter now, does it?"

"I . . . I guess not."

"What happened to Frank?"

Jolene drew air deep into her lungs, this time without pain. And when she let go the breath, the stream of her whispered words spilled out with the force of an unstoppable river.

Moments later, when Alice and Jolene stood in silence, the outside door came open and Zassy came into the kitchen. She smiled, opened her arms, and Alice nearly collapsed against her.

"It's wonderful," Alice said. "It's so wonderful."

"What?" she asked.

"Frank," Alice replied.

"Yes." Zassy appeared flustered. "Yes."

Alice stepped back, hugged the letter to her breast.

And Zassy's eyes darkened. "Yes. But we'd best talk about it later, I guess. We have to get dinner on now. You go on and see your mama and daddy and we'll talk later." She forced a smile.

Alice kissed Zassy on the cheek, then turned and kissed Jolene's cheek, too, before handing back the letter and leaving through the swinging door.

A silent moment after she'd gone, Zassy turned on Jolene, her eyes narrowed.

"You ain't got no right," she said. "You took that letter out of my Bible."

Jolene looked to the floor. "I was just so happy and I–"

"I can't forgive you for this, Jolene."

Jolene looked up. "But Alice is family. Ain't she got a right to know?"

Zassy snatched the letter away and tucked it into her skirt pocket.

"Why are you so worried?" Jolene went on. "When I told her, she–"

"That's just it," Zassy snapped. "That's just what I'm talkin about. And what do you think's gonna happen if she tells Mister Samson about this? You never think things through."

"Alice ain't gonna tell nobody. I don't know what you're gettin so–"

"Shut up, Jolene." She turned her back.

"Zassy, don't do this." Jolene placed a tentative hand on her shoulder.

But Zassy lowered her voice and shrugged the hand

away. "I'm sorry for ever lettin you near me," she said. "And I don't know if I can–accept it anymore, Jolene. Us. What does God think about us?"

"He loves us," Jolene replied in a whisper tinged with certainty. "You know that."

"Does He?" Zassy turned to face her. "Does He really? Or have you and me just convinced ourselves He does?"

"What do you mean?"

"I mean, all them strange feelins you say you get sometimes around Frank. You ever think maybe God's tryin to tell you somethin? A human bein can make up all sorts of lies about things, about the way things are supposed to be, but it don't mean shit to God unless we–" She stopped, her eyes filled with ugliness and hurt.

"Zassy," Jolene said. "God *is* love."

Samson and Ronnie looked up when Alice entered the parlor.

"Well," Samson said. "How's my little girl?" Dapper in a red velvet vest, he wore a thin-striped dinner jacket: white and maroon woven together to create the illusion of pale pink. His mustache was shorter. And grayer.

"Fine, Daddy." Alice hugged him and pulled away. "How are you?"

"Couldn't be better." He stabbed at the air with his cane. "Why, I was just tellin Ronnie about how me and Claude took on this Union case back before Christmas. Now don't you go lookin so surprised, honey. You know I never was a big proponent of the labor unions after all that horse shit last year. I–" His discourse came to an abrupt halt as he looked over Alice's shoulder.

Marie stood in the parlor entryway. She wore the same black evening dress she'd worn to the Republican convention in Baton Rouge five years before, her hair pulled back. But her eyes were vague, her skin waxy.

"Mama." Alice moved to Marie's side and hugged her with a satisfied smile.

"Well," Samson said. He straightened the line of his flamboyant dinner jacket and turned to Ronnie. "So. You think somethin's gonna come of all this horse shit in Germany?"

"Yes, sir," Ronnie replied.

The room seemed alive for a moment, but the conversation was forced: a polite rendering of familial animation.

"Excuse me, sir." Jolene stood in the doorway, a tremulous smile at her lips. "Dinner's ready whenever y'all wanna eat."

Samson lurched forward, grace in his otherwise pronounced limp. He raked Marie with a sidelong askance as he made his way past and into the dining room.

Along the dinner table sat steaming bowls of greens and mashed potatoes, two wicker breadbaskets and two bowls of rice. Everyone took a seat as Jolene carried in a glazed ham and set the platter near Samson.

"Can I get y'all anything else, sir?"

"No," he said. "What you got for dessert?"

"There's strawberry shortcake if anybody's got a mind for it." She offered a half-hearted smile. "The good berries. Canned last summer."

Samson nodded. "You go on now."

So she did.

Samson reached for the bowl of stiff rice as everyone began to fill their plates. A moment later, he said, "So how's your schoolin comin along, honey?"

"Fine," Alice replied. "I'm pullin a three-point-eight this semester. But the algebra's givin me some trouble."

"Algebra." Samson chuckled. "Who the hell needs it?"

"My professor, Doctor Goldstein, said–"

"Goldstein?" Samson interjected. "He a Jew?"

She nodded. "He's a good teacher."

Samson fell quiet. At the opposite end of the table, Marie raised a trembling water glass to her lips, never once meeting the gazes of those around her. Ronnie reached for another helping of the mashed potatoes, plopped three large spoonfuls on his plate.

Alice took a deep breath. "Did you know Frank's preachin now?" she said.

Silence.

"They call him Bayou Jesus," she went on. "He's givin a sermon on Easter Sunday. I'm gonna go hear him."

The solid vein in Samson's forehead began to throb. He lowered his voice and turned to Ronnie. "Nope. Sure never thought I'd raise a nigger-lover."

"Daddy!"

Samson turned to Alice. "You associate with niggers, you *are* a nigger-lover."

Alice opened her mouth to retort, but he shushed her with a raised hand.

"Everybody's got a place," he said. "You know that's what I always say." He lowered his hand to the table. "Someday you'll realize you're better off."

"Better off than what?"

"Better off leavin things like they are." Samson leaned back in his chair. End of conversation.

But Alice challenged him. "You can't win this one, Daddy. You can't win this time by cleverly tellin the truth."

"I'm not talkin about this anymore," he said.

Alice looked to Ronnie. "What do you think?"

Ronnie's gaze wavered between Samson's glare and Alice's stare. "About what?" His cheeks flamed.

"Go on, boy," Samson said. "You tell her she's wrong."

But he remained silent.

"Ronnie?" Alice pleaded. "Say somethin."

"I . . . really don't think it's such a good idea," he finally said. "I mean, to go–"

"You think Daddy's right?"

"I–"

"All of you think I shouldn't go hear Frank because he's colored, that's what it is. But don't you see? Don't you see that it doesn't matter what color mouth the Word comes from, as long as it's God's?"

"You don't know what kind of trouble that nigger's stirrin up," Samson said. "He's gonna be up to his eyeballs in horse shit if he ain't careful."

"But why can't you accept the fact that–?"

Samson leaned forward and thumped the table. "Because he's a nigger!"

Alice bit her lip.

"Just let it go," he said.

"Why?"

"What do you think's gonna happen if people start believin a nigger who thinks he's Jesus? It's just another plot to try and take over."

"Take over?"

"Mmm-hmm." He nodded.

"Take over what?"

"The world, honey. The world."

"I always knew you were biased," she said. "Impious. But–"

"Un-what?"

"A non-believer."

"That the kind of horse shit they're teachin you in school?"

Alice muffled a bitter laugh. "You just don't see it, do you?"

"See what?"

"See beyond the world you're livin in."

"What else is there? You want niggers takin over the whole parish? The whole state? The whole country? Is that what you want?"

"Daddy, the world you're livin in is dead and gone."

"I don't wanna hear it."

"That's right, you only hear what you want to, don't you?"

Samson clenched his fists. The vein at his forehead throbbed harder.

"You're bein preposterous, Daddy, so close-minded and–crazy."

"What?"

"You're crazy, that's what I said. Thinkin Frank's tryin to take over the world. Do you know how–crazy that sounds? I think you're afraid of him. And I think it's because you're not . . . right with God."

"Crazy am I?" He pointed at Marie. "Crazy as that?"

"Daddy, how can you?"

Samson drew a massive breath. "I am so *goddamn* tired of all this *goddamn* talk about niggers and–God–I could just–"

"What, Daddy?"

"Never mind." He leaned back in his chair again, looked down table, and saw Marie pouring from her flask.

"Marie!"

She raised precipitous eyes over the glass trembling near her lips.

"You disgust me," he said.

Alice stood. "I don't know how you've lived with this man as long as you have, Mama. I'd've been gone a long time ago if it was me. I'd be behind you all the way if you just got up and walked out and never came back."

Samson lurched to his feet. "You stay out of things that don't concern you, understand?"

"Concern me? My mother shouldn't concern me?"

He nodded.

Alice turned to Marie. "You go on and have a drink, Mama, I know why you do it, who makes you do it." She looked back to Samson. "It's him. That man who sits on the Legislature and rubs elbows with Governors and Congressmen. But what does it mean to a man who's so blind to the fate of everybody around him? Wouldn't it be wonderful if nobody knew what hate was, Mama? If we all weren't just smotherin in it, if we all weren't just drownin?"

"I don't ever–wanna hear you–say things like that again," Samson seethed. "You forget I'm your daddy?"

She lowered her head. "I feel so sorry for you."

"Alice?" Ronnie spoke for the first time in minutes as he, too, stood.

She raised her eyes to meet his gaze, tears pushing against the brim of her lids. "I don't know you anymore," she whispered.

"Don't cry," he soothed.

"I don't want to cry," she said. "Believe me, I don't want to." She turned away and left the room. A moment later, Ronnie followed.

And Samson turned back to Marie. "I hate you," he muttered.

The veil of injustice, like the sticky-sweet haze of Louisiana in summer, hung thick about Alice and Ronnie as they drove back to New Orleans next morning. From there, Ronnie went on to Biloxi alone.

With no men allowed in the girl's dormitory, Alice didn't see Ronnie for several days, although she knew he was the one who kept calling.

The week before Easter, he caught up to her on her way to class. She told him she was late, had to go, hadn't worked things out yet. He asked her to come to his fight at the arena the following night and maybe they could get together afterward. She said she'd think about it, then quickened her step.

But the next night, she sat high in the bleachers amidst the roars and the cheers, anonymous in a sea of faces, lost in an ocean of indecision. She saw the grim set of Ronnie's jaw, the animal glint in his eyes as he bounced on the balls of his feet, preparing for the brutal dance of the boxing ring's tragic theater.

The bell clanged. Ronnie rushed center. Struck the LSU boy with his trademark right cross. Bestial cries rose from the crowd.

But something happened in the second round. Ronnie lost focus, his defense grew awkward. The LSU boy smashed a glove into Ronnie's nose and sent him sprawling backward onto the canvas.

The referee began to count.

And a great cry rose from the crowd:

"Get up! Get up! Get up!"

And he did. He wobbled to his feet, dizzy, lurched forward with another cross. And the roar that followed reached a frenzied pitch.

Alice came to her feet, caught up in the excitement. She stamped her feet and cheered. But when she saw the shock of blood at his face, saw his swollen nose, her heart went out to him. She couldn't watch. She picked her way down the crowded bleachers and into the bright lobby lights.

The bell clanged again.

A collective despair rose from inside. The end of the match. And, no doubt, Tulane's defeat.

She found a deserted bench outside and waited as the doors flew open to disgorge hundreds of flushed, excited faces.

Some time after the crowd had thinned, Ronnie walked

out: showered, swollen and bruised. Alice stood, and gently kissed his cheek.

"I'm sorry," she whispered. She gazed into his eyes. "And I don't want to wait anymore."

"What do you mean?" he asked.

She pressed her head against his chest, heard his heart beating fast. "I want to take care of you. I want to–"

"Why?" he asked. "I mean, why now?"

"Because I love you," she said. "Because I can teach you. Because we can teach each other." Her arms fell from his shoulders. She clasped his hands. "Come on," she said, and pulled him down the lamplit walkway.

"Excuse me, sir." Zassy stood in the doorway of Samson's study holding a silver serving tray.

"What?" He looked up from the pile of briefs on his desk.

"Will you be takin your lunch in here again today, sir?"

"Bring it on in."

Zassy moved into the room and placed the tray on the edge of his desk. "Will there be anything else, sir?"

Silent for a moment, Samson finally drew breath and said, "I know you know how I feel about Alice goin to see your boy."

She lowered her gaze to the floor.

"I want you to understand that . . . ." He trailed off.

"Sir?" Zassy raised her head.

He cleared his throat. "I want you to know that I'm just lookin out for her, understand? I want you to know that I feel the way I do because . . . ."

She nodded, whispered, "I understand."

"I knew you would." He sighed. "You're not like Jolene. You understand about things, the way things are, the way things are supposed to be, don't you?"

She didn't speak.

"You're . . . somehow . . . better than most of your kind. I know I haven't always been the easiest man to deal with, but I want you to know that I do regard you as, well, above most."

"Thank you, sir." A lifetime of sublimation, of place and differentiation, manifested itself in a ponderous weight upon her heart.

"You're probably aware that–" A distasteful expression washed Samson's face. "Aware that things haven't been right between me and Missus Boudreaux for many years now."

She didn't reply.

"You know a man can get . . . lonesome."

Still, she remained silent.

"What I'm tryin to say is–" Samson cleared his throat again, stood, and limped from behind the desk. "How long's it been since you . . . ?"

"Sir?"

"Shit." He sighed, moved closer. "I thought maybe–" His gaze seemed to penetrate her own.

Angry, yet unexpectedly accepting of his advance, reason spelled redemption for her in his arms. Zassy tried to speak, but found she couldn't.

"I thought if you had a mind to . . . ." His hand trembled toward the warm cushion of her breast.

"Mister–"

"Shh. Hush now."

Run away. Save yourself.

Let him. Save yourself.

"No," she whispered.

* * *

When Zassy fled, left Samson furious and embarrassed, he clenched his fists until the blood raced to his head in a nauseous surge.

He picked up the telephone, dialed, said, "How's your good eye today, Jimmy?"

"Huh?" Jimmy Hazard asked.

"There's a little somethin I need you to see to," Samson said.

Ronnie's body woke first, alive with Alice's fleshy memory. For the last few nights, she hadn't wanted to risk sneaking into his dormitory, didn't want to risk smuggling him into hers, either, so love was sloppy and feverish on the coupe's vinyl.

Ronnie opened his eyes and yawned. He padded barefoot from bed down the hallway, dialed her number, and waited.

Three rings.

She always picked up by the second.

Five rings.

She didn't leave for class until ten, but was always up by seven. Seven-thirty at the latest.

He hung up. Dialed again.

Six rings. Seven.

Why wasn't she picking up? Where was she?

He dialed Shirley Anderson.

"Shirley? It's Ronnie. Have you seen Alice this mornin? She wasn't in her room so I thought she might be there."

"She didn't tell you?"

"What?"

"She left around six this mornin."

"Where?" An alarm resounded in his ears, much like the brassy clang of the bell at ringside.

"I don't know. Last night she said she was leavin this

mornin. Guess she went home."

"But she didn't say anything to me about it. She wouldn't skip Algebra."

"I'm tellin you all I know, kid. Take it easy, I'm sure it's not like she's gonna have an affair or somethin." Shirley snickered.

"Huh? What?"

"Never mind." She sighed. "I was makin a joke."

Samson had a terrible day. He should have been satisfied with himself for what he'd done, but he wasn't. Hell, what harm could there be in stirring up a little fright in the niggers, as a reminder, so to speak? Somebody had to make sure ideas like a nigger-Jesus didn't get out of hand. And when Zassy heard the news . . . .

The telephone rang. Samson swiped it up.

"Claude, I told you–"

"It's me, sir. It's Ronnie."

"Well, what brings you to callin at this hour, boy?"

"Alice."

"Huh?"

"Could you have her call me when she gets in? I don't have a class until noon, so I'll be around the dorm."

"Is she supposed to be comin home?"

"I think so. If you'd just have her call me, I'd appreciate it."

"Oh, sure, I'll do that."

"Thank you, sir."

"How come you ain't comin? Got another fight this weekend?"

"No, sir. She didn't tell me she was goin home."

Samson sighed. "I sure hope she ain't comin back to argue," he said.

Ronnie offered a meek chuckle, and rang off.

* * *

Jolene peered out the train window to a grassy field rushing by, remembering a day long ago when she and Zassy stood beside a similar field: younger, bound to each other by the baby they took turns carrying for miles on end.

Zassy had stayed home. Said she couldn't bring herself to go to Breaux Bridge. It wouldn't be right, she felt, to punish Frank with her presence: a sinner not yet come to terms with God for all her misgivings.

Jolene knew that if Zassy didn't face up to things soon, she'd lose everyone that loved her. But maybe she had the right to worry about things, though, because wasn't being aware of sin enough for the Lord to know you were sorry for it? Wasn't Zassy's suffering repentance enough?

Jolene opened her Bible and read:

For the Lord Himself shall descend from heaven with a shout, with the voice of the archangel, and with the trump of God: and the dead in Christ shall rise first: Then we which are alive and remain shall be caught up together with them in the clouds, to meet the Lord in the air: and so shall we ever be with the Lord.

Now it made sense. Was it the Lord she'd met so long ago over Frank's crib? Or an angel? Was Frank the source? Where in the Bible did it state the color of Jesus' skin? The voice of reason said that from a geographical standpoint, His flesh must have been dark. And nowhere did it state the color of His skin upon the Second Coming. If God was white, did that mean a colored man could never be God-like? God created man in His image, so with man being so many different colors, might not God be, too?

Maybe she'd know the answers to all her questions when she next saw Frank, when she heard him preach this weekend. And maybe she'd be caught up in the clouds again, too.

A faint breeze, a tepid draft, touched Jolene's warm cheeks. A gentle hand grazed her shoulder, then another seized her heart.

An unseen force passed through her: quivering, flickering, dying.

She took two deep breaths, and let go her last.

Sunday: 1963

Miss Zassy stopped. The sign we passed said Breaux Bridge. She closed her eyes.

"Things could have turned out different, you know," she said. "Things could have turned out for the better, but how was anybody to know?" She opened her eyes again. "Nobody would have expected that to happen to Alice. Nobody."

Miss Zassy picked up a flimsy cardboard fan, although earlier she'd been adamant about not using the air conditioner. A picture of Jesus leading a flock of sheep to a lush, green valley was stapled onto a thin wooden handle. Hotter, more uncomfortable the higher the sun rose, my collar had grown too damp, too tight, and some time ago, I'd loosened it and rolled up my sleeves.

"She was just so full of good," Miss Zassy went on. "I think she wanted to believe there's good in everybody, so she just shut her eyes to the things she didn't wanna see."

She took a deep breath. "Well, Mister Samson told me that mornin that Alice was comin home, but along about the middle of the afternoon when she ain't showed, I could tell he's worried, thinkin maybe somethin happened.

"I was changin the sheets on Miss Marie's bed when Mister Samson comes in. He screams, 'Where's Alice?' and I said I don't know, and he said, 'You're a lyin nigger, Zassy'. He said I'd best tell the truth, because he'd know if I was lyin. I said I didn't know, and I wasn't lyin, neither. Then he told me to get out, and that he'd better not catch me listenin around doors or spyin on people again or I'd be sorry.

"Before I even got to the stairs I heard him start in on Miss Marie, screamin, 'Where's Alice?' like she should know, but all she could do was cry. She didn't know nothin. Nobody did then. But Samson thought he knew, and that's all that mattered to him.

"I heard him come downstairs later, off to his study, talkin on the phone with the door wide open like he wanted me to hear what he said. 'Get me Ronnie Mitchell', he said."

* * *

Frank opened his Bible and read aloud:

"Another parable put He forth unto them, sayin, 'The Kingdom of Heaven is likened unto a man which sowed good seed in his field: but while men slept, his enemy came and sowed tares among the wheat, and went his way. But when the blade was sprung up, and brought forth fruit, then appeared the tares also."

Ten members of Christ's Hope Church lined Simon Duchane's small kitchen. The rest of the congregation milled outside, picnicked on the lawn.

"So the servants of the householder came and said unto him, Sir didst not thou sow good seed in thy field? From whence then hath it tares? He said unto them, An enemy hath done this. The servants said unto him, wilt thou then that we go and gather them up? But he said, Nay; lest while ye gather up the tares, ye root up also the wheat with them. Let both grow together until the harvest: and in the time of harvest I will say to the reapers, Gather ye together first the tares, and bind 'em in bundles to burn 'em: but gather the wheat into my barn."

Frank laid his Bible aside and looked up.

"Jesus said this is the way of the world, evil and good growin together until the end of the ages. But let us not be weary in well doin: for in due season we shall reap. The thief cometh not, but for to steal, and to kill, and to destroy. Jesus said I am come that they might have life, and that they might have it more abundantly.

"So be ye angry and sin not: let not the sun go down upon your wrath: neither give place to the devil. Love your enemies, bless them that curse you, do good to them that hate you, and pray for them which despitefully use you and persecute you. And do not be deceived: God cannot be mocked. A man reaps what he sows. The one who sows to please his sinful nature, from that nature will reap destruction."

Simon Duchane leaned his six and a half foot frame against the kitchen door, listening to familiar words become new, as if being heard for the very first time. Well dressed in blue pin stripes hung from broad shoulders, he held a fedora at his side and shuffled his wing tips. His jaw was set at a slight angle from an old accident in the shipyards of Saint Louis, but his sideways smile captivated, and his intelligence charmed.

Simon remembered the day he'd discovered Frank, 'the man of miracle', the man called Bayou Jesus. No more than a boy, really, with long, unkempt hair and a thick beard, holding an audience captive with the sound of his voice. Men, women and children surrounded him in a loose circle beside the bayou. Frank's words weren't remarkable, it was their delivery:

"And Moses said before the Lord, 'Behold, I am of uncircumcised lips, and how shall Pharaoh harken unto me'? But in the New Testament Jesus says, 'Ye are the light of the world. Let your light shine before men, that they may see your good works, and glorify your Father which is in heaven'.

"So, brothers and sisters, it's unimportant how we praise the Lord, how He uses us, as long as we seek to do His gracious biddin. You, sir." He laid a hand on an elderly man's shoulder. "I can see by the calluses on your hands you've worked hard all your life and broke a lot of soil with these fingers. I can see seasons of crops come and gone in your eyes, feel the pain in your back, bent from years leanin toward the earth, but carryin the strength of the Lord in your heart."

"Yes, yes." The silver-haired man bowed his head.

"What question burns in your heart, sir? What knowledge do you seek from the Lord?"

The old man raised his shaky head. "Knowledge?"

"Yes, sir. Only through knowledge will you grow closer to God, then He'll help you by showin you the right way to go about curin your aches and pains. Why, every day He opens a hundred doors for the man who's eager to learn, who yearns for knowledge. For only through knowledge can we have truth, and only through truth can we have God.

"Don't rely on others to work miracles for you, sir. You show your faith and strength by your frail body. Your bent back says you've spent a lifetime in accomplishment. Thank the Lord for it and ask Him how to ease your pain. He'll show you. He'll point you in the right direction."

Frank gazed around the circle.

"So many of you have come today to ask God to heal you. Your bodies, your minds, your souls. But ask yourself this: ain't it too easy just to pray for God's help? Ain't it too easy just to say, 'Here I am, Lord, make me well' without even tryin to help yourself first? The good Lord gave us minds to use. He gave us minds to think and to question the mysteries of life, the unexplainable things in the world, because in their unexplainable nature is where we find His presence."

Frank moved around the circle, looking into each pair of eyes, until he came to Simon.

"And some of you come today not to be healed of body, but of mind. Some of you know what I'm sayin when I talk about the quest for knowledge, the thirst for more it brings a man once he starts learnin."

Simon shifted under Frank's gaze. A great love, a simple wisdom–like an electrical shock–grasped at the nerve-endings along the length of his great stature.

"You, sir, have a loud voice cryin out in your heart, urgin you to serve the Lord in a way you're not comfortable with, am I right?"

Simon nodded. His heart beat faster.

"And what is the Lord tellin you to do?"

Simon choked, gathered the splinters of his voice. "I

believe He's tellin me to preach."

"What makes you resist?"

"Because I'm scared."

"Of what?"

"I'm a giant, but I'm afraid." Simon cast his gaze quickly around the circle. "When I'm in front of a whole group, I just freeze and I end up feelin a foot high. I prayed He'd help me overcome it, but He ain't yet."

"Believe me when I tell you that you have nothin to fear," Frank replied. "God'll give you a voice when He feels it's right, not before. So continue to spread His word the best way you know how. Show Him in everything you do."

It was that moment Simon realized why he stood on the edge of the bayou, drawn to the man who promised salvation, but not through miracles or easy answers. Frank could be Simon's voice.

When the worshippers dispersed, Simon found himself alone with Frank. He asked to walk with him, and they strolled along the bayou, remarking at the beauty of God's creation, delighting in each other's company: that indefinable oneness men rarely feel when in the presence of another man.

Late that afternoon, when they returned to the spot where Frank moored the Drumson's skiff, the two had struck up a fine friendship and a mutual bargain. With Simon's know-how, he would help bring the Word to a greater number of people. And Frank would be his voice . . . .

Like now. Like the voice pulling Simon back to his kitchen and the present as Frank finished:

"But as it is written: Eye hath not seen, nor ear heard, neither have entered into the heart of man, the things which God hath prepared for them that love Him. But God hath revealed them unto us by His Spirit: for the Spirit searcheth all things, yea, the deep things of God. Amen."

* * *

Alice checked into a tourist court and ate at the diner next door. After a fitful nap, she changed into a white cotton blouse and a pair of denims, then checked at the office to see about cab service, but learned there was none.

"I got a cousin, Miss," the withered manager said. "Name's Jake. He can take ya where you're goin."

A simple man in grease-stained coveralls and cap, Jake's gaze betokened a childish naïveté.

"Where ya headed, Miss?" he asked.

"Out along the river, I guess," Alice replied. "Bayou Teche. I'm lookin for Christ's Hope. I'll pay you."

"That's a colored church, Miss."

"I know."

But he only shrugged and said, "All right."

Some time later, Jake's mud-speckled pickup truck inched alongside the bayou on a rutted dirt road.

"That's the Teche," he said.

But Alice saw no signs of life. "Where's the church?"

"Down here."

Tall trees thickened on either side of the road as the truck continued on. But moments later, the dense verdure fell away and revealed a small structure, square and unremarkable. Alice gazed beyond the church to the river's opposite shore, to the blazing heavens, where the sun drowned in flames.

"You gonna get out or somethin?" Jake said.

"No."

"How come you're wantin to come out here, anyway, Miss?"

"A friend of mine's gonna be preachin here Sunday and I wanted to know how to get here."

"You could have asked me then, not any need in just drivin out now."

But how could she explain it to him when she hardly understood things herself?

"I told you I'd pay. For both times."

"Who's your friend?"

"Frank is–" Alice paused. "They call him Bayou Jesus."

"Bayou Jesus? Really? You know him?"

She nodded.

"They say he works miracles. They say . . . ."

"What?"

"That he's–like–" Jake's somewhat childish eyes grew troubled.

"What?"

"Well, my cousin, Manny, he's what you call a thinkin man. He told me a story once about when Jesus come back to the world a long time ago. He's in jail, see, and there's this other fella, too. It's when people was gettin killed for bein Christians or somethin, I think. Well, this fella tells Jesus He's a liar, that He ain't who He says He is, and this fella says even if Jesus was Jesus, He's already given him the power to–deny Him–or somethin. That this fella can do whatever he wants, even kill Jesus without feelin no guilt, see."

Alice had grown uneasy as Jake talked. "What makes you think of that?"

"Well, Manny says it's kind of like that with Bayou Jesus. He says if this feller thinks he's Jesus–"

"He doesn't think that."

"Manny says some people think He is and some people think He ain't."

"What do they say?"

"About what?"

"About him."

"Like what?"

"Like–"

"You mean did somebody–? No. Manny didn't say anything about anybody doin Him harm. The way I remember it, Jesus was let go at the end of the story."

* * *

The silence grew caustic, erosive, like a canker spreading its poison.

Ronnie tapped his fingers against the steering wheel, stared through enormous pines on either side of the road, reaching toward a violet ribbon of sky overhead.

He pulled up to a gas station as the lights flickered off.

"We're closed," an attendant said.

"I only want directions," Ronnie replied.

"Where you headed?"

He told him he wasn't sure. A church? And then he said the name; tested it, tasted the way it sounded in his mouth, like bitter coffee: Bayou Jesus.

"Say, you with them other fellers?" the attendant said.

"What others?" Ronnie asked.

Some miles outside town, Alice spied oil lanterns flickering amongst the trees, a group of people crowded into a small yard.

"Slow down," she said.

"What is it?" Jake eased onto the brake.

"That house over there." She saw the backs of heads in the warm glow of the lanterns, their attention directed toward a porch where a tall figure stood beside an even taller man. "That's him! It's Frank!"

Jake stopped. Alice opened the door and climbed out, peered into the growing dark to see distant black faces all turned toward her, countless eyes staring back.

"Miss?" Jake asked. "You ain't gonna go up there, are you?"

"Of course," she said. "Come on."

"No."

"Why not?"

"I can't."

"Hello!" came a voice. "Can I help you?"

"If you wanna go, then go," Jake said, a marked panic in his voice. "But I ain't."

"Hello! Are y'all lost?"

"Shut the door!"

The handle wrenched from Alice's grasp. The truck lurched away. The red glow of taillights disappeared down the highway.

"Miss?"

Alice turned toward the sound of the voice, saw a tall shadow all but obliterated by night devouring day.

"Is this–? Is that Frank Potter?" she asked.

An infinite breach of wariness preceded a hesitant reply. "Yes, Miss. It is."

"I've come to see him," she said.

"Who are you, Miss?" The tall shadow moved closer.

"Alice. Tell him it's Alice Boudreaux."

"Why, yes! He's spoken of you. Come on up, Miss Boudreaux. He'll be real glad to see you. I'm Simon Duchane, welcome to my home."

The murmur of voices in the yard rose to a mixed volume of relief from some, quiet trepidation from others, as Alice and Simon approached the gate. He led her through the group gathered close on each side–staring–toward the house, and into the glow of the lanterns.

Frank stood on the porch. He didn't move. His eyes were masked by a curious emotion. Did he tremble?

"Frank," Alice said, and smiled.

Frank noticeably swallowed. "Alice," he said.

* * *

Bayou Teche. Christ's Hope stood half in shadow, half in moonlight, beside murmuring waters. Headlights grazed its whitewashed wood. Ronnie shut off the engine and sat, lights glaring against the building. He listened to the chorus of the night: the cicadas chirping in the trees, the frogs croaking along the water. Then he shut off the lights.

A young black man extended his hand and welcomed Alice. Then five hands reached out to her as Simon chuckled and said, "Oh, he was a figure, all right, Miss Alice, comin out of the fog in the early mornin light with a paddle in one hand and a Bible in the other. Looked just like the Savior comin over the water."

Everyone agreed.

But soon, people began to leave.

"I can take ya back in town later," Simon told her. "I'm sure you two got a lot of catchin up to do. Excuse me." He disappeared inside.

Frank moved to sit on a wooden chair, Alice leaned against a post. For a moment, it seemed a living entity fed off the quiet between them.

Finally, Frank said, "Does your daddy know you're here?"

"No," she told him. "Nobody knows, not even Ronnie."

He didn't reply.

"Frank?"

"Yes?"

"Sometimes . . . Sometimes I don't know if I can love Daddy anymore. Sometimes, I don't know if–Ronnie–"

"Of course you do," Frank said. "They just need

direction, that's all. That's why you're here, to give it to 'em."

Alice smiled.

"They'll learn from your example someday," Frank said.

Alice moved closer. "Tell me about what happened to you." Her voice grew eager. "Tell me what it felt like. Tell me–"

He bowed his head. "It's hard to explain." When he looked up again, Alice stood directly over him. He took a deep breath. "What do you feel when you pray? Do you feel like God's listenin? Do you feel like He's in the same room, standin over your shoulder?"

"Yes," she said. "At least, I want to believe it."

"Then just imagine prayin and openin your eyes and lookin over your shoulder and really seein Him. Imagine seein Him so clear you could touch the hem of His garment. Imagine the air is alive, swarmin like bees over a field of flowers in June. That's what it feels like."

"You've seen Him, haven't you?" Sudden tears pressed against her eyes. "What is He, Frank? Who is He?"

Frank took her hand. "I wish I knew. I wish I did, but I don't. And I've really only sensed Him. I know He's the spirits of everybody on earth, I know He's more than that, too. Greater. He *is*. He's you and me both, right here, right now."

"We are, aren't we?" she murmured. God lived in Frank's eyes: a God demanding her embrace, upon Whom she'd waited her entire life.

But a swift and fleeting pain washed Frank's face.

"Frank? What is it?"

"Excuse me." He stood.

"Are you all right?"

He didn't answer. He walked off the porch and into the moonlight.

But Alice followed. "Frank?"

He stopped beside the river, but didn't turn to face her as she came to his side.

"Do you remember?" she said. "Do you remember that night when we sat by the river and you were tellin me about your doubts?"

"I remember."

"The water reminded me, the way it sounds, the way it's so loud you can't even hear it at all. Do you remember what I told you then?"

"No."

"I told you everybody had doubts, that you wouldn't be human if you didn't."

"That's right."

"Are you still doubtin?"

He turned toward her. "What?"

"It's so hard not to, isn't it?"

"What do you mean?"

"I mean, we can only really guess at God, can't we? But do we really understand Him? Does anybody? And if nobody does, how can we not doubt? Even you. I still see doubt. I know, because I know you. At least, I know who you used to be. You're hurtin, I can tell. What is it?"

She closed the distance between them, between what she knew to be God and her ability to be God-like.

"I doubt," she said. "I believe, too. My doubt is part of my belief, I guess, because without believin there'd be nothin to doubt."

"Yes," he whispered, so low that the faint hiss of the word grew indistinguishable from the rush of the river.

"What are you doubtin?"

"Why He would send you here."

"What do you mean?"

"I mean, why did He send you here to tempt me?"

"Tempt?" she whispered. "Is there always a greater

plan in what people do, or are some things left up to us to decide?"

"I believe He guides us in everything we do," he said.

"I believe He points us in the right direction." She stepped next to him, pressed her breasts close under his ribcage, felt him tremble against her. "Would God deny the love of two people, the love that brought them together? Not if He was the God of love and life, surely not if He–" The sense of living flesh, warm against her own, of abundant life coursing through his body, forced by the heartbeat of life itself–thus God–beckoned her to follow.

"'Let us love one another'," she said, "'for love is of God; and everyone that loveth is born of God, and knoweth God'. Moses married an Ethiopian and God told the people who were scornin them it wasn't sinful."

The force of his hands closed over her arms, pinned them at her sides.

"Alice! What are you sayin? It's a sin."

"Why? God promises happiness."

"Ultimate happiness, Alice. He put us here to suffer, to find our own way to Him, 'cause His happiness is the reward, not earthly happiness."

"No, Frank, you're wrong. If we didn't have happiness on earth, how could we believe in somethin that denied it to us? There'd be no happiness, no joy in worshippin Him."

"I'm sorry." His hands slipped from her sides.

"For what?"

"For holdin you that way."

"Then make it up to me," she said.

"How?"

"Baptize me."

"What?"

"The bayou. I want you to baptize me in it."

"Alice, I–"

"I want Him. I want to feel *your* God and to know *His*

joy."

He fell silent.

"Frank?"

A pool of water, trapped in an artery of Bayou Teche, lay beside Christ's Hope. Frank took Alice's hand and led her into the tide, cold against her bare feet. When the water swirled waist-high, he turned her back facing shore, toward the reflection of silver moonlight lapping against the banks.

"Are you ready?" he whispered.

She trembled, offering him the power of life and death, trusting him to take her into death and bring her back out into a new life. She nodded.

Frank raised his voice: "But if we walk in the light as He is in the light, we have fellowship one with another, and the blood of Jesus Christ His Son cleanseth us from all sin."

From shore, Ronnie heard the water accept her, saw Frank's shadow redeem her from the tide, then bend to embrace her.

"How do you feel?" Frank whispered.

Alice gazed into the darkness, drawn toward tiny points of light flickering amongst the pines: fireflies?

"Do you feel it, Frank?" she murmured. "Listen. It's like the whole world is just . . . holdin its breath."

Part Three

Ghost

Immediately after the tribulation of those days shall the sun be darkened, and the moon shall not give her light, and the stars shall fall from heaven, and the powers of the heavens shall be shaken: And then shall appear the sign of the Son of man in heaven: and then shall all the tribes of the earth mourn, and they shall see the Son of Man coming in the clouds of heaven with power and great glory.

–*Matthew 24:29-30*

. . . . the fog swirling across her vision like a snowstorm smells of smoke full of angry and excited voices full of ghosts floating-flapping in the glare of so many bright lights gathering around her like a dream and–

a sharp crack at the side of her face jolts her into awareness as a foot descends on her breasts her stomach her hips so many feet kicking and pummeling so many her body won't allow itself to feel the pain or–

she shuts her eyes tight against the maelstrom the humiliation as strong hands push her swollen broken lips against the earth turning the dust to blood-mud as an alien sensation grows between her legs pricks of splinters biting at her inner thighs

shove it up her cunt

and the scream tears from her throat as the wood leaps up into her splinters devouring her from inside and she can only see frank hanging from one of the low branches of a gnarled tree

then another's face ugly in its familiarity rears up before her sick and pale amidst the laughter the terrible jubilant laughter rising in the air twisting like a veil of fog-smoke obliterating the night and the flames of the burning cross

and she screams
roooooonnnnnniiiiiieeeeee . . . .

Sunday: 1963

What goes through a mother's mind when she outlives her child?

At times, Miss Zassy walked ahead of me, and I merely observed her. She carried herself with dignity, infused with an uncommon strength but for those whose lives demand they be stronger than most. Why did she want to come–here, of all places? What drove her to make such a dubious pilgrimage?

We'd made our way along the banks of the Vermillion River, searching for the sight where Christ's Hope once stood. The locals informed us that the church building wasn't there anymore, but we'd found the remains: a broken concrete foundation.

"I ain't never seen the place 'til now," she said, "but I . . . ."

"What?" I asked.

"You'll just think it's the ravin of an old woman if I tell ya."

"No I won't."

"Sure you will. Don't all young folks think old folks like me are half crazy? Out of their minds? Slow? I did when I was a girl. Didn't pay no mind to old folks. They were just a nuisance, gettin in my way. But the older I got, the more I realized 'old' is an age a person ain't reached yet."

I smiled.

"I think it's a holy place," she murmured.

I didn't reply.

"See?" She caught my gaze. "You think I'm just a foolish old woman, don't ya?"

"No," I said. "Of course it's a holy place. Wouldn't any parent think that?"

"You mean, if they'd lost a child?"

I nodded. "No matter what the circumstances surrounding the death of a child, the place where their soul left the earth, no matter how–violent–no matter how– It's the place where their child's soul departed from this world, where the child met God."

"You're a good man." She clutched the small package tight against her breast. "I knew it when I met you. That's why I let you bring me up here. There ain't hardly no good men left."

"I appreciate that."

Miss Zassy turned to stare out over the river and said:

"'But the day of the Lord will come as a thief in the night, in which the heavens shall pass away with a great noise'." She took a deep breath. "'And the elements shall melt with fervent heat, the earth also, and the works that are therein shall be burned up, and the heavens, bein on fire, shall be dissolved'." She turned back.

"That's how it was. That's how it was when Frank died. The whole world was just like a bomb waitin to go off. Me, I was so worried about where Jolene was, I–" She broke off and averted her gaze. "Funny how when the people cause you the most grief ain't with you no more, funny how you miss 'em that way." She looked in my eyes. "Probably think I got what I deserved, don't ya?"

"Ma'am?"

"Probably think since I loved another woman that my grief is God's punishment, don't ya?"

"No, Ma'am."

"Most folks do. Most folks wouldn't think twice about tellin me I'm bound for Hell–not because of what you might think, but because I don't regret what I did. But that's where they're wrong. The Bible says, through Jesus' death, we have redemption through His blood. Even the forgiveness of sins. So I know He forgives me even for the not regrettin. I made up my mind a long time ago about things."

She turned her back, stood straight, showed me that strong woman's spine. "She was my strength, you know. When she went, when I found out, when I read in the paper about the woman they found on the train outside Lafayette, I knew it's her. You can't spend most of your life with somebody and just not know. I told Mister Samson I'm sure that's Jolene, but he said, What you want me to do about it? She done run away. Ain't none of my business. Wouldn't even let me go claim her."

Miss Zassy turned again to face me. "But what if I had? What would I've said, huh? If somebody asked me what relation I was, what would I've said? My sister? No. I would've had to tell the truth. There comes a time when people have to. It's a shame people can't show their love for one another, ain't it?"

I didn't reply.

"Day later I hear about Frank. Hear people's goin crazy around Breaux Bridge, burnin and lootin and such, but the police got things in hand. The police found him. Said the house was still smokin, tire tracks all over the yard in a big circle. Must have lit it all up with their headlights. Say Frank's hangin from an oak tree. And it's so quiet it's like the end of the world." Her eyes glazed over with a picture only her imagination could supply. "Day after, his body was lost."

"Lost?"

"Disappeared."

"How?"

"I mean just plain gone. Like the mornin Mary Magdalene come up on Jesus' tomb and He's just gone."

"What happened?"

"Some say he got up and walked away, some say God rose him up from the dead, resurrected him."

An oppressive stillness grew between us, cold as a snowstorm in July.

"Did anybody ever–?"

"Find him? Yeah."

"Well?"

"Patience, young man. There's a lot more lost that day than just my boy, and that's hope."

"What happened to the others?"

"Man Frank's stayin with, Duchane, his wife and little baby girl, not more than five years old, they burned up in the house fire. Duchane, he got away."

"What about Alice?"

"She's gone."

"Where?"

"Somehow or another, she managed to get herself to the neighbors, quarter mile or more on up the road. She crawled. Said she's about dead when they found her, scratchin on the back door like a hurt animal, beggin for somebody to help her. Said she was just an open wound. Bruises and black eyes, broke nose and ribs. Just a pitiful animal, not even a human bein no more.

"When the man on the radio talked about the girl in the hospital, I told Miss Marie I thought it was Alice. But she didn't say nothin. Didn't even look at me. Mister Samson, he didn't talk, neither. He didn't say nothin. People don't down here. People don't never talk about things like that. They're afraid to.

"But I knew there'd come a day when I'd have to, when I'd have to say somethin. I'm an old woman. I can't carry stuff like that around no more. And me, I'm the one who went to her when I saw her Mama and Daddy ain't gonna. I just packed my bags and struck out, right for all that trouble in Breaux Bridge. What was keepin me where I was? Everybody I spent my whole life lovin was gone."

"Did they ever catch the ones responsible?"

"Didn't I just say people don't talk?"

I bowed my head.

Miss Zassy sighed. "Guess it don't make no difference now, though. Besides, I don't know anybody knows who Alice Boudreaux is no more, who she used to be."

I raised my head.

"Sure enough, I found her in the Lafayette hospital. After what's done to her, I don't know how she managed, except for the grace of God. She was bleedin so bad inside cause somebody–put a cross–like the crosses they was burnin–small one, ya know–put it up inside her."

"God."

"But it's amazin how strong them things can be sometimes, after what's done to it. Just holdin on, fightin for life. It's a wonder."

"That she made it?"

"That It made it." Miss Zassy's gaze darkened, her cheeks flushed ashen. "We knew she gonna make it after a couple days. But she didn't have no idea, though, nobody did, that she's gonna have a baby."

VI

Shrapnel

Alice lay broken and bruised in the hospital at Lafayette, unable to move of her own will. Poked and prodded, so many needles came to burn in her flesh. So many, that the gray-blue streaks down her arms grew longer every hour.

She called for her mother. She screamed Ronnie's name. Frank's name. Nurses came into the room, starched uniforms swishing against their white-stockinged legs. Then the brutal taste of steel from the bit shoved into her mouth, jaws clamped around it to keep from swallowing her tongue.

And more needles.

And no one she ever cried out for came.

Alone.

Then the doctor told her she wasn't alone: life grew inside her. Did she cry? She didn't know. He said, 'It's alive. But there's a problem'. Something about what had been done to her. Something about what had been done to It.

'I can't do it', he told her.

It?

'Get rid of it. Too much at stake. Can't risk my– But I know someone who can do it for you. For It. For Its sake'.

Then she cried until the convulsions started, until they shoved the bit into her mouth again, before the needles found the raw flesh along her arms once more.

'Alice? Can you hear me? Alice'?

Through the black mass of her mind, it comes: a single voice striking a familiar chord.

'Honey, can you hear me? Do you know who I am'?

She hears the voice from below dark waves, where she drowns, where brackish waters fill her lungs. Yet she can't die, can't release herself into death.

She remembers a river, gentle hands dipping her into the tide . . . .

Where she now struggles, unable to free herself, unable to swim to the top, for air, for release.

God. Where are You . . . ?

She fights the water, so thick it's like moving in a dream. Arms and legs pinion. No use. No matter which way she turns, no matter how hard she fights to break the surface, she can't. No light. From above. Or from below.

Am I gettin closer? Am I goin the wrong way?

'Alice'.

Help me! I'm tryin to reach you, but I can't!

'Honey, wake up. It's me. It's Zassy'.

Zassy?

But the water is, after all, too deep.

Samson slammed down the phone.

"Don't tell me about it," he muttered. "She's not my daughter."

* * *

The sound of a rope, stretched to its limits, pushed and tugged by the wind. The resistant groan of branches. The crackle of leaves in the breeze.

He fights to open his eyes. But he can't. He tries to loose his hands from behind his back. But he can't.

The sounds of steel slicing through taut rope.

Then a wonderful sensation of flying, like a bird, through billows of clouds in a bright blue sky.

He doesn't know where he is or really just who he is.

I'm Ronnie.

He knows his name is Ronnie, but it has no meaning.

Then there are voices:

Looks peaceful, don't he?

Uh-huh.

What gets into folks you think?

Who can say? Too late for answers now, though.

And Ronnie wakes.

The summerhouse is always so cool under the shade of two big willows. Off to itself. How she laughs and plays there. Jones sanded down the split rails until they're smooth as a baby. And can he play that banjo! For hours and hours sometimes. Until well after dark. But Beulah made special candles to keep the mosquitoes away . . . .

. . . . and Marie runs after Daddy again as he carries something into the summerhouse again. And yet again, he doesn't see her.

And she runs up the rock steps, sees Jones has strung deer jerky to cure, and she can't wait for a big salty piece to chew on.

Daddy?

In the shadows of the summerhouse, Daddy turns.

Daddy?

Take it, Marie. Daddy's big girl. Do it for Daddy.

Again he hands her the gun.

And again, she takes aim. At him. For him.

But she can't do it. Not again.

This time, it will be different. This time, she turns the gun on herself.

Bayou Jesus explodes in thunder and

Sunday: 1963

"Couple nights later, Alice came to. When she saw me, somethin in her just sort of broke. She was cryin and askin me about Frank and Ronnie, about her mama and daddy. I don't remember just how it was I told her about Mister Samson hangin up on me, or even if I told her right then. But even as delicate as she was, I think she knew. But her mind wouldn't let her body know. Know what I mean? If her mind was to let her body know, it might not have had the strength to rebuild itself.

"Ain't that how most folks manage? Denyin things about themselves, about other people? It's hard for folks to admit to themselves the truth. And that's the way it was with her, she wasn't ready to accept things yet.

"She begged me to get her out of there, but I told her she had to stay and rest and let the doctor look after her. She tried to prove to me how strong she was, started sittin up and sayin, 'See? Ain't I told you?'

"You know why she wanted out of there, don't you?

She was ashamed, that's what. That's when she told me about the baby and made me promise not to tell. Not to ever let on to nobody where she was. Not to say nothin about that baby.

"When I told her about Jolene, and that I ain't goin back, I think she made up her mind then, too. Think that's when her mind started lettin her body know about what was done to it, who's responsible.

"Few days later, once she get her strength back, we just walked right out the front door. I bought her a dress in town–well, what's left of town. She slipped it on and took my arm and we just walked out. Didn't have no idea where we were goin, though, what we were gonna do. Walkin down them broken sidewalks, all the store windows boarded up like it really was the end of the world. And we walked and walked 'til we ended up in that place up on Bayou Teche."

Miss Zassy turned away from me, took a deep breath, then let it go.

"I remember the night he came. Oh, Lord, that raggedy thing. It'd always be there to remind us about that night. I prayed to God it wouldn't live. I did. I prayed He'd take it, but He never did.

"When Alice saw him, she started in cryin for a long time, and I think she knew what Hell was then. I think she understood everything about the past and about the years to come. The misery. She didn't want nothin to do with it for a long time. I thought about loosenin the cord while Alice was sleepin, but I couldn't bring myself to. I've seen a lot of new babies, but I ain't never seen nothin like what I rocked and looked after while Alice would just sit and look the other way."

Miss Zassy stopped, turned back to face me.

"There. I said it. Said what I promised I wouldn't never."

* * *

His eyes were huge, forever pleading for her mercy from within his shattered body. His mouth was a slash. When he tried to smile, his lips could only curl into a sneer. His hips tapered away to withered legs, to a waste of flesh and bone: impossible for him to ever walk normally. Instead, he used his hands, dragging the useless part of his anatomy behind–like some sort of animal. He begged and whined like an animal, because he couldn't speak.

But Alice never wondered about things that might have been. Loving him as he was, was all she could do.

She couldn't work outside the secluded shack they called home, because he demanded constant attention. She and Zassy took in sewing and laundry, but never let anyone inside, never let anyone know about the monster kept chained to his bed once he'd grown too strong for his own good. Too strong to keep from hurting himself and them if they didn't chain him.

He hated the shackles, clattering against the rusted bed frame as he writhed on the mattress.

But sometimes, they still took him outside. Because he loved the water. Loved to splash at it and lap it. Like a dog, Alice once thought. But always, they leashed him.

For seventeen years.

The soothing, sweet rush of the river wound through the trees outside Baby's window, pierced the fine mesh of mosquito netting which made most of what he knew of the world.

out

He struggled against the cuff, tight against his twisted hand. It fell free. He turned onto his side. Mama was still asleep. And Othermama wasn't home yet.

Baby worked at the remaining cuff. Mama would be mad if she knew. Chain scraped metal. He froze. Closed his eyes to a squint.

But Mama still slept.

out

He twisted his wrist against the shackle again. It, too, slid free.

Baby eased himself onto his hands, the strength of his shoulders supporting his weight. He shuffled across the floor, opened the door, then hopped off the porch. He gathered speed, and broke into a trot.

J.R. and Woody took their daddy's new red pickup without his permission. Neither old enough to drive, J.R. at least had a permit, 'which is all you really need anyway', he told his younger brother.

Tall for his age, with dark brown hair and eyes, a low brow and thin nose, J.R. had already outgrown his classmates. His lanky, lean frame anxious for manhood, impatient for the rest of him to catch up, he was apt to forget that what his stature made up in definition, his mind lacked in maturity.

Four years younger, Woody's crew cut grew blond and fine. Plump, blue-eyed and snub-nosed, Woody leaned toward learning about the world, whereas J.R. lived it. And the few years separating him and J.R. made a world of difference: brothers whom were once friends, but were now strangers and natural enemies.

J.R.'s right cowboy boot hit the floor and the truck tore up the open highway outside Lafayette. Windows down, the roar of the wind made it impossible to discern what staticky song played on the radio.

"Slow down!" Woody yelled. "What if we get stopped?"

J.R. laughed, but eased off the gas.

"Where we goin?" Woody asked.

"Hell," J.R. said. "I don't know. Out. Takin a look around. Fishin."

"Where?"

"On the bayou, Woody Woodpecker."

"Don't call me that."

J.R. laughed.

"Why don't we just go back home?"

"We're goin fishin."

"Where?"

"I don't know. There!" J.R. turned the wheel sharp. The truck balanced on two tires for an instant, then rocked back onto the dirt road with a metallic shock.

"Daddy's gonna kill you," Woody said.

"Shut up."

The road turned muddy, choked with weeds.

"Where we goin?"

"Fishin, now shut up!"

But by the look on J.R.'s face, Woody knew his brother had no idea where he was.

The road came to a Y; J.R. turned right. Mud splattered the grill, speckled the windshield with sludge.

"Daddy's gonna kill you," Woody said again.

But J.R. ignored him. His face grew pinched. He pulled the truck onto a patch of grass and stopped.

"What are you doin, J.R.?"

"Goin fishin!" he snapped. "Shut up and get out."

"I don't think–"

"Shut up! Get the goddamn fishin rods out of the back and shut up!"

Woody pulled himself from the truck, sneakers squelching in the soggy earth. He took the poles in one hand, the tackle box in the other, then ran to catch up to J.R., already across the clearing near the wood. J.R. walked too fast–on purpose–but Woody fell in step behind, out of breath and quiet. J.R. bent his lean body like a green twig, ducked under a low-hung branch, and disappeared.

Woody caught up to him several minutes later, but only because J.R. had stopped.

"You hear that?" J.R. said.

"What?"

"Over there." J.R. pointed to a clump of brambles. "Think it's an alligator?"

"Gator?"

J.R. laughed, then grew deadly serious. "Why in hell did I bring you along, Woody Woodpecker? You're a pain in my ass, you know that?"

"Why you gotta be so mean to me, J.R.?" Much as he hated it, a tear escaped Woody's eye.

"You're a cry-baby, too."

Woody sank to the ground in defeat. "I hate you, J.R."

"I hate you worse," J.R. spat. "I–" He stopped, turned, cocked his head, said, "Did you hear that?"

"Stop it, J.R.!"

Too quiet.

Alice blinked away the veil of sleep.

And her heart leapt in her chest.

Empty bed. Open door.

She bolted outside to find an empty yard, then fixed an anxious gaze on the bayou.

That's when she heard screams from deep in the wood.

"Get up, Woody!" J.R. yelled.

Woody raised his head, furious at being taunted

further. "Leave me alone, J.R.!"

"Woody!" J.R. backed toward the trees in the direction they'd come.

Woody heard a low grumble at his back, and froze. He peered slowly over his shoulder.

It wasn't an alligator, but it *was* a monster, with hands like claws–reaching for him–and a mouth on sideways. Woody screamed, tried to crawl away, but it grabbed his legs and Woody went face-first into the mud.

"J.R.!"

But J.R. had disappeared.

For hours it seemed to go on as Woody screamed and screamed and–

"Stop it!" A woman's voice.

Woody clawed for the ground in front of him, tried to shake its clamp off his legs.

"J.R.!" Woody screamed. "Roooooonnnnnniiiiiieeeeee"

J.R. emerged from the opposite line of wood. He carried a tree limb.

And brought it down on its head.

It turned loose of Woody, howled, and rolled onto its back, blood streaming in its eyes.

The woman screamed.

Woody rushed beside J.R., the woman rushed to its side. She stared up at J.R. and a strange look crossed her face: confusion?

"Ronnie?" she whispered.

Then it began to howl louder–like an animal.

"Come here!" the woman called.

But J.R. snatched at Woody's collar, and they fled in horror through the trees.

"Where the hell have you been?" Ronnie shouted. It hadn't been fate that brought Ronnie Mitchell back to Lafayette, but reason: business and family. Reason was when a man made up his own mind about things, without the interference of the subconscious or cluttered beliefs in something like spirituality. And, too, reasonable men believed less in God as they grew older; level heads just seemed to come at such a cost.

J.R. and Woody stopped. Caught sneaking into the house. Woody was covered in mud from head to foot.

Ronnie turned on J.R. "Boy, you're in deep shit. You better start explainin."

But J.R. couldn't speak–until his father began to advance. "I'm sorry. I'm sorry about the truck. Really. I–"

The forceful smack of an embittered man can be harsh, but the slap of a boxer given up dreams, can be lethal. The jolt sent J.R. into the wall. He didn't buckle, but staggered, dazed.

"You're goddamn right you're sorry! I oughtta blister your ass right now!" He twisted J.R.'s arm behind his back.

J.R. cried out.

Woody shrieked and fell to the floor of the kitchen where he started to sob uncontrollably.

"What the hell's wrong with him?" Ronnie loosed his grip.

"That's what I'm tryin to tell you, Daddy," J.R. said, near to tears himself. "Somethin tried to kill Woody."

"What?"

"We went into the woods outside town. Up on Bayou Teche. We was goin fishin. And– It tried to kill him, Daddy. It did."

"Where? What?"

"Bayou Teche, Daddy."

"Where on the Teche?"

"I could–show ya."

"What was it?"

"I don't know. But there was a woman, too."

Ronnie lowered his brow. "You tellin me the truth?"

J.R. nodded, fought coarse tremors erupting in his body.

"Can you show me where?" Ronnie's eyes demanded agreement.

J.R. nodded again.

"Go tell your mother to take care of Woody." Ronnie let go J.R.'s arm. "She's upstairs. Worried sick about you. About what you've done. About what you're turnin into. Tell her we're goin for a drive. Tell her we're gonna go see just what you've done to my new pickup truck."

Panic.

It had been over two hours since Alice chased after the boys until they'd disappeared, over two hours since she'd returned to the clearing to discover Baby missing, too.

"Oh my God," Zassy whispered when Alice told her. "You mean he's lost?"

"Up there." Pressed against the muddy passenger door, J.R. pointed.

"You sure?"

He nodded.

Ronnie slowed the truck and turned off the highway, bounced through muck and mud, weeds. J.R. told him to go right when they came to the Y.

"That's where we pulled over," he said, and pointed.

Ronnie parked, climbed out of the truck, and claimed a rifle with adjustable sights from behind the seat.

"Come on," Ronnie said.

J.R. opened his door and stepped out.

Through birch and pine, dodging branches, swiping at leaves and mosquitoes, the ground hissed under the soles of

Ronnie's and J.R.'s boots.

Several hundred yards into the wood, the trees opened overhead.

"This is it," J.R. said.

Ronnie moved through the tall grass to the middle where it lay beaten down. He examined it. "Yep. Blood. Wounded. Couldn't have got far."

But half an hour later, Ronnie muttered, "I don't think your monster's around here, boy."

"He's gotta be here somewhere," J.R. said.

"You ain't lyin to me, are you?" Ronnie grabbed J.R.'s arm.

"You're hurtin me, Daddy!"

Ronnie let go. And J.R. stumbled backward over a rotten stump.

"Watch where you're goin," Ronnie said. He fished a cigarette from his breast pocket and lit it.

J.R. pulled himself up, swiped at the mud on his arms.

"Wash." Ronnie pointed to the water with the rifle's barrel.

J.R. moved to the river's edge and bent down beside a cluster of branches hung low over the water. He splashed at his arms.

Then saw it.

Its head bobbed just above the water's surface in a circle of algae beneath the branches. Still, it wore that demonic, sideways grin.

J.R. jumped back, landed on his buttocks. And screamed.

"Where is it?" Ronnie called. "Where is it?"

But J.R. only pointed.

Rising from the algae on thick arms. Pulling itself

forward. It looked like a man, but it couldn't be. This did not fit into the natural order. This couldn't exist.

Ronnie raised the rifle as it came ashore on twisted limbs, dragging stubs for legs. He leveled the sights between its eyes and the rifle seemed to burn with a heat of its own.

Mesmerizing, the way it looked at him, cocking its head from side to side to discern what it could about him–as if it were actually thinking.

It's human.

"Oh, Lord." Ronnie's mouth drew tight. "Deliver us from evil."

And he fired.

Two, three, four times the sounds of shots rang out.

Alice ran from the porch, leapt over mire, up and over debris in pursuit.

As the clearing where the nightmare had begun fell behind, she heard the distant roar of an engine coming to life.

And when she finally broke the cover of wood and came out onto the road, she saw the truck retreating.

Two heads: one boy, one man.

The man turned to the boy.

Even in twilight, Alice saw him smile.

And she knew who he was.

Baby was still alive when she found him, still alive with that same determination for life he'd possessed in the womb, although four shells had been emptied into him.

Alice cradled his head in her lap, the left side gone, jelly leaking onto her denims. Then he rolled his eyes, huge even in death, and moved his crooked mouth as if to speak.

* * *

Neither Alice nor Zassy could sleep. They sat outside the glow of a small oil lamp, silent after futile attempts at conversation. There wasn't need of consolation, as if all the words that might be said were already understood.

At five o'clock, as Zassy finally drifted into a thin sleep, Alice walked outside. She found a shovel and started to dig.

Stained with mud, she walked down the overgrown path to the main road, the air undulating with the quick heat of new day–as if something strained to break through the very canvas of reality.

The car slowed to a stop a few feet in front of her. She climbed in.

"Where to?" the young man asked.

"Town." She stared ahead through the windshield at the imitation world outside.

"Lafayette?"

She nodded.

He tried to make conversation, but when she wouldn't respond, he fell silent.

"This is as far as I go," he said, then dropped her at a gas station.

She found a pay phone, thumbed through the directory. And had an answer within minutes.

She walked.

An hour and a half later, she saw it: a large, single-story red brick. No different from the rest along the street. It shimmered in the noonday heat, itself a part of the reproduction that passed for her world. She stepped up to the front door and knocked.

* * *

"Ronnie, there's someone here to see you," Susan called. Tall, with shoulder-length black hair, his wife stood in the kitchen doorway, her dark eyes uncertain.

"Who is it?"

"She says she's a friend of yours. She says her name's Alice."

Disbelief ferried Ronnie to the living room where an impenetrable silence lay in wait–like a monster, feeding off the oxygen.

She was the same. Age hadn't touched her. However, her eyes had paled, grown older than his.

"Ronnie?" Susan said.

He struggled for his voice as his stomach tensed, his body absorbing the shock.

"Alice? Is that–really you? My God, it's– What happened to–? We were worried, you know. Everybody was." But he didn't know what else to say. No way to prepare for this. No way to make anyone understand about the black hell into which a man can plunge.

"Stop it," Alice said.

Ronnie fell silent.

Alice turned to Susan. "Would you please excuse us?"

"Ronnie?" Susan pleaded. Her gaze searched his face for a sign of explanation.

"Go," he said, and turned away.

A moment later, Susan had gone–but no doubt none too far.

"You think I can't be here, don't you, Ronnie?" Alice's gaze anesthetized his own. "But I never left. My life just stopped at Breaux Bridge. And when life just stops for a person who's still breathin, it's as good as bein dead. How could you kill him?"

"I—I didn't." He choked on an anxious flood of words. "I didn't kill him. I didn't."

"I saw you."

"I know!" A sickening cyclone began to spin inside him. "Don't you know? Don't you know I only–? I can't tell you how–what it's done to me all these–"

"I'm not here about the past, Ronnie. I'm here about my boy. Your son. Do you know you killed our boy yesterday?"

A rush of dread bristled over the nape of his neck, caused the very roots of his hair to tingle.

"I saw you. I saw you at Breaux Bridge, and I saw you yesterday, too."

He turned away from her, ashamed and despicable: for never coming forward, for denying her. "That–thing?" he said. But there weren't any more words. His gaze darted about the room, fixed on familiar objects–*Look* magazine on the coffee table, pictures hung precisely–the way a condemned man will fixate on something insignificant while being led to execution. "How?" he said.

"Do I have to remind you how babies are made?"

Ronnie shook his head. "It was his. It was Frank's. I saw the two of you."

"Frank never touched me that way," she said. "I wanted him to, but he couldn't. I wish it had been his child, at least maybe then I might have really loved him. Do you know that every time he opened his eyes, he loved me with the life shut up in his body? And do you know that I couldn't ever really love him back because of what he reminded me of? Do you have any idea what that's like?"

"Alice, I–"

"But I'm here to release you, Ronnie. From your pain. Just like Bayou Jesus was there for me." Her eyes grew vacant, her voice caressed the room like a cool summer breeze. "I once wondered about the meanin of God, now I know we make our own."

Her eyes hinted at a blissful suspension of reality, her movements those of a dreamer, slow and fluid, reaching for the pistol snug inside the waist of her mud-stained denims.

The wind picked up, whipping at the deserted lawns, rippling the earth in forever changing patterns. At this early hour, a man stood on Susan Mitchell's front porch, gazing through a narrow crack the door afforded him. He wore a khaki blazer and pants, pressed a cream felt fedora to his skull, anchoring it against the wind.

"Go away," Susan said, drained and disheveled. "I've already made my statement. Leave us alone." She shut the door.

The man walked away from the front stoop, but felt eyes boring into the back of his head. He looked over his shoulder, noticed the sway of lace curtains in the bay window as they settled back into place.

Before he reached the door of his rental car, he heard a voice, muted and tossed by the wind. He turned back and saw a young, frail boy standing alone at the west corner of the house.

"How's that?" the man called.

"Are you on TV?" the boy said, black crescents of sleeplessness under his eyes.

The man glanced at the bay window, then moved into the yard, but the boy retreated around the side of the house.

"Hey, kid! Wait up!"

He rounded the corner, came face to face with him: cropped blond hair, pale blue eyes, and a terribly pale face. "What's your name?"

"Woody."

"My name's Don," the man replied. "Are you all right?"

He shook his head.

"What's the matter?"

"Mama told us not to talk to TV people."

"I'm not on TV."

"Who are you?"

"I'm a reporter. I work for a newspaper in Bossier City. I was hopin to talk to your mother, but I guess she's not feelin well, either."

"She's been sick, too."

"What's the matter with you, Woody?" Don stepped closer. "You can tell me."

"I've been dreamin about it again," Woody murmured. "About monsters. Mama says there ain't no such things, but I saw it. J.R. did, too. I dream about the woman, too."

"The one who hurt your daddy?"

He nodded.

"Is she the monster in your dreams, Woody?"

"No."

"Then what is? What happened?"

Woody's gaze darted side to side. He opened his mouth, but before he could speak, another voice called out:

"Woodrow Alan Mitchell!"

Susan stood at the opposite corner in the back yard, hair unkempt, green bathrobe rumpled, eyes swollen from crying.

"You get in here right now, young man!"

Woody bolted for the front of the house.

"You son of a bitch!" Susan turned all her fury on Don. "I'm callin the police! Leave us alone!"

And he retreated, her voice slithering after him, promising jail time and lawsuits.

Once in the rental and out on the main highway, he noticed thunderheads on the horizon, so he rolled down the window. The air grew cool, heavy with the promise of rain. He wondered if he'd remembered to bring along an umbrella. He wondered about the boy who couldn't sleep, because every time he closed his eyes he saw a monster.

He wondered about the woman he first saw at the Lafayette Parish jail, wearing a severe gray uniform. She hadn't uttered a sound at first, but then her sobs echoed off the concrete and steel when she told him her incredible story, when she said Jesus told her to do it.

He wondered about secrets, great and small, these people kept.

The first splatters of rain speckled the windshield as he made his way downtown. Ahead, lay the criminal justice building, where the trial of the State of Louisiana versus Alice Boudreaux began at ten o'clock.

UNION, JUSTICE AND CONFIDENCE

surrounded the pelicans on the State Seal.

The low whisper of voices at Alice's back became a river: rushing, alive, ever shifting. Every seat occupied by unfamiliar gazes, what breathing air remained was stifling and sour, even with the three large fans humming overhead. Societal downfall demanded such intimacy.

She wore a long brown skirt, a matching blazer over a yellow blouse, a small amount of make-up. Her lawyer suggested she wear heels. He said it would behoove her to look as feminine as possible.

Then the announcement:

"All rise."

So help you God?

So help me God.

* * *

Susan Mitchell, the statuesque widow, took the stand. Only after she took her oath did she peel back her black mourning veil.

"Just tell us what happened on the date in question, Mrs. Mitchell: June 16, 1955. That Saturday mornin." Thurgood Pinochet played fair unless crossed. Tall and thin, the prosecutor wore wire-framed lenses that gave the illusion of his eyes being larger than they actually were.

Susan drew breath, ready to give a practiced recount, ready to tell the story yet again of the day her husband was murdered.

"Woodrow–he's my youngest–was at the door. I asked him who it was, but he didn't answer me. When I went to the door, I saw her."

"Who?"

"Alice."

"Mrs. Mitchell, do you see Alice Boudreaux in the courtroom today?"

"Yes, I do."

"Could you point her out to the jury, please?"

Susan raised her hand and pointed at the defendant.

"Mrs. Mitchell," Warren Tibbets cross-examined. At fifty-five, with robust cheeks and jowls, he'd been in the service of the city his entire adult life, and court-appointed attorney for twenty-five years. "Do you love your children?"

"Of course," Susan replied.

"And can we assume you'd do anything for them?"

"Yes."

Tibbets drew breath, swelled up his chest. "Would you say you might even kill for your children?"

"Objection, your Honor!" Pinochet snapped. "What line of questionin is this?"

"Sustained." The Honorable Emile Chouard turned to

Tibbets. "Counselor, is this valid?"

"Yes, your Honor."

"And what do you hope to prove?"

"That Alice Boudreaux acted in self-defense. A momentary lapse of reason." He turned to the jury. "A mother's instinct to protect her child. The child Ronnie Mitchell murdered. A child that belonged to him."

"My husband didn't murder anybody," Susan said.

"You are the deceased's son?" Tibbets questioned on the second day, another bleak and rainy afternoon.

J.R. nodded, his palms sticky and hot. He wore a new suit, and his mother made him oil and part his hair.

"I want you to tell the court what happened the day before your daddy was murdered. Can you do that? Can you tell us just what took place?"

"My brother, Woody, and me." J.R. swallowed. "We took Daddy's pickup to Bayou Teche. Somethin–I don't know what it was–attacked Woody. And I–knocked it off him."

"Could you be more specific? Could you describe what it was that attacked your brother?"

"I don't know. It was like a boy, only it wasn't."

"Like a boy, ladies and gentlemen of the jury," Tibbets said. "Only it wasn't."

Late that afternoon, Detective Roy Ray Willits testified for the prosecution. No remains were found, he said. But there were signs: a shallow grave by the river, washed away from a rainstorm, Bayou Teche claiming whatever had been inside.

And the bed. It looked like someone had been chained there for a very long time.

* * *

On the third morning, bright and warm after two days of rain, Zassy took the stand.

"Tell us about your son, Miss Cole," Tibbets prompted.

"Frank was a preacher, sir," she replied. "Folks called him Bayou Jesus."

"And isn't it true that he was, how shall I say, blessed?"

"Yes."

"Could you tell the court what happened?"

"He–wept. The blood of Christ."

"Counselor Tibbets," Judge Chouard interjected. "Will you approach the bench?"

Pinochet stepped up to the witness stand on the fifth day:

"Miss Cole, may I read a verse to you from the Bible?" He glanced at Tibbets, then to Chouard, but when neither man voiced objection, he turned back to Zassy.

"Certainly," she said.

Pinochet opened the Bible. "'And Jesus answered and said unto them, Take heed that no man deceive you. For many shall come in my name, sayin I am Christ; and shall deceive many'." He raised his strikingly large eyes behind the thick lenses, and stared directly at her. "This is the book of Matthew. Twenty-fourth chapter, verses four and five."

"Counselor Pinochet," Chouard said. "We are not concerned with the notion of the resurrected Christ."

"Yes, your Honor," he replied. "But you see, what we're dealin with here is metaphysical."

"How?"

"Because if we're to understand the defendant's

involvement with this man, we must know what kind of person he really was."

Over the weekend it began to rain again, carried into Monday, the sixth day of the trial. More anxious reporters, turned away at the door, huddled under umbrellas outside.

"Most of the worst crimes in history have been committed in God's name, ladies and gentlemen," Tibbets said, pacing in front of the jury box. "And this case is no different.

"We have here a woman who believes an outside force instructed her to seek revenge for the murder of her child, a child she claims to be Ronnie Mitchell's. You must keep in mind that she's experienced a great tragedy that drove her into retreat, both physically and mentally. Who's to say voices didn't tell her to do what she did? In the mind of a–"

"Where are you goin with this, Counselor?" Chouard interjected.

Tibbets looked up at the judge. "To prove Alice Boudreaux justified her actions in this manner. To prove she wasn't sane in those moments when she took Ronnie Mitchell's life. To prove he bore responsibility for this heinous act." He turned to the jury. "And to ask for forgiveness and mercy in her sentencin. 'Who shall give account to him that is ready to judge the quick and the dead'?"

"State your name."

"Doctor Alan Sawyer."

Pinochet stepped up. "Doctor Sawyer, we've heard Frank Potter performed certain miracles at your hospital."

"Supposedly."

"And the name of the hospital?"

"It's the National Leprosarium at Carville."

"And how many years have you been at the Leprosarium?"

"Twenty-six."

"So you were in residency on the night in question?"

"Yes."

"And what did you see?"

"There were people crowded around him. People I think wanted to believe he could heal. A mass hallucination maybe."

"And did he heal?"

"I–can't answer that."

"Were any of the patients better afterward?"

Sawyer thought for a moment. "Yes. Some."

"And do you believe it was caused by spiritual healin?"

"I–don't know."

"You were conductin some experiments of your own at the time, weren't you?"

"Yes. Sulfones. They're now commonly used to treat leprosy."

"And the effect of the drugs?"

"Remission."

"Like the patients in remission who were supposedly healed?"

"Yes."

"Isn't it true that all the patients who did get better, who were 'healed', were test subjects?"

"Yes."

"No further questions, your Honor."

On the seventh day, Alice took the stand:

"Ronnie Mitchell was the father of my son. I saw Ronnie the night Frank was killed, and I saw him the day he killed our son."

"But you believe you were instructed by spiritual forces to murder Mister Mitchell?" Pinochet questioned.

"I– Yes. No. It was–"

"What, Miss Boudreaux? It was what? Is it because Ronnie Mitchell spurned you?" Pinochet turned to the jury. "Is anyone else in this courtroom as unsure about the father of the child as I am? Does anyone wonder if it really weren't Potter's boy?"

"He was Ronnie's."

"You are under oath."

"I know." Alice's gaze locked on Pinochet's.

"Well, Miss Boudreaux," Pinochet said. "The only thing we seem to have gathered so far concernin whether or not you are capable of murder is simply this–correct me if I'm wrong: Jesus instructed you to kill Ronnie Mitchell."

Alice remained silent for a moment, then leaned forward and murmured, "It's not me who's on trial today, is it, Mister Pinochet?"

Sunday: 1963

"I will use the foolish to confound the wise," Miss Zassy said. "And professin themselves to be wise, they became fools." She sighed. "Everybody's just blowin smoke. It was all just a show. Of course Frank knew he weren't the Son of God. And everybody that knew him knew it, too. But I do believe God worked in him." She turned away and stared out over Bayou Teche. "They argued another day and a half, each one tryin to come up with the answer to Who God was, what God was. But they never did. And you know why?"

"Why?"

"Because nobody knows about God that way. Nobody. Folks can only just guess at it.

"Day the verdict come down, I saw Alice outside the courtroom, between all them cameras and microphones. Her eyes caught mine for just a second, and I swear she was smilin. Because she was free of it now. She got twenty years with time off for good behavior. But she's still up there at the corrections house in Texarkana. And that's it, I guess. Except for that Mister Duchane."

"Yes?"

"I remember the day I looked up, it wasn't long after I settled back in Lake Charles to be near my old church family, and there stood the tallest man I ever saw. He said his name's Duchane, and I tried to remember where I heard that name before. Then it came to me, Frank mentionin him in that letter. That's when he gave me this." She held out the package in her hands.

"He said he was the one that took Frank's body that night, said he couldn't bear to let him go. Simon Duchane was Frank's disciple, see. Said he sat up with him three days before he started to smell, waitin to see if– Well, that's when he did the crematin. He tracked me down after all these years to give me what's left of my boy. Said he's a preacher now. And that's all there is to tell."

A breeze stirred between us, cool, with the promise of night.

"Miss Zassy?"

"Yeah?"

"Thank you for letting me bring you here today."

"You're welcome." Her gaze found the river. She tore the paper from the package, said a silent prayer, and opened the box to release the ashes to the elements.

I watched in the vain hope that I might indeed catch a glimpse of God. I wanted to hear the sounds of oars lapping at the water, hear the creak of a boat out of sight in the evening fog settling over the bayou. I wanted to see a tall man gripping a paddle in one hand, holding a Bible in the other. But there came only the murmur of the water as the ashes floated out of the shallows and into the rushes, out to the main flow, where they began to separate, and to dissolve.

"Now he's dead, really and truly," she whispered. "'I shall go to him, but he shall not return to me'."

"Are you all right?" I stepped closer, admired her profile poised against the dying sun and the river.

"Fine." She thought for a moment. "But if you ever do

tell the story, if you ever write about everything, just say one thing."

"What's that?" I asked.

"That it don't matter about all that other," she replied, "about whether my boy was or wasn't who people wanted him to be. The important thing is that he was different things to different folks. Like you and me. Like God Himself. See, it don't matter who you love, just as long as you do love. And it don't matter about color or religion, or anything else like that, either. Because we're all equal in the end."

"Yes, Ma'am." My voice faded under the rush of night. "Are you ready to go now?"

"Yes." Miss Zassy sighed. "Yes I am, Woodrow. Take me home. We both need to get some sleep."

ABOUT THE AUTHOR

M.G. Miller has authored eighteen novels and numerous short stories spanning several genres, and has received awards from Arkansas, Oklahoma and Louisiana states for his work. He is the fiction editor for Surreal Magazine, published by Cavern Press, as well as the editor of the press' Surreal imprint.

Before his life literally became "surreal", Miller was a tour guide in a cavern, worked with abused and neglected children, and drew world maps in a building with no windows. He lives in Fayetteville, Arkansas, and is currently at work on a new novel.